THE DEATH OF
A CELEBRITY

AN AMOS LEE MAPPIN MYSTERY

THE DEATH OF
A CELEBRITY

AN AMOS LEE MAPPIN MYSTERY

HULBERT FOOTNER

COACHWHIP PUBLICATIONS

Greenville, Ohio

ISBN 1-61646-263-9
ISBN-13 978-1-61646-263-5

Cover: Red curtain © Deyan Georgiev; Hulbert Footner (George H. Doran Co., 1921)

CoachwhipBooks.com

CONTENTS

Chapter One   7

Chapter Two   12

Chapter Three   16

Chapter Four   20

Chapter Five   24

Chapter Six   29

Chapter Seven   40

Chapter Eight   47

Chapter Nine   55

Chapter Ten   61

Chapter Eleven   70

Chapter Twelve   76

Chapter Thirteen   84

Chapter Fourteen   89

Chapter Fifteen   95

Chapter Sixteen   100

Chapter Seventeen   107

Chapter Eighteen   112

Chapter Nineteen   118

Chapter Twenty   123

Chapter Twenty-One   129

Chapter Twenty-Two   134

Chapter Twenty-Three   137

Chapter Twenty-Four   141

Chapter Twenty-Five   145

Chapter Twenty-Six   147

Chapter Twenty-Seven   154

Chapter Twenty-Eight   161

Chapter Twenty-Nine   167

Chapter Thirty   175

Chapter Thirty-One   186

CHAPTER ONE

Miss Gail Garrett, accompanied by her elderly maid, Catherine, was on her way to dinner at Gavin Dordress'. She was appearing in Robert Greenfields' play, "White Orchids," at the time, and the party had been arranged for Sunday night to suit her convenience. She had not the expression of one who is looking forward to a good time. In the seclusion of the car her beautiful face was tense and stormy. When the cab stopped she saw several men with square boxes hanging around the apartment-house door, and she hesitated before getting out.

"Press photographers? Who do you suppose tipped them off? Gavin wouldn't."

"They always seem to know where you're going to be, Miss," said Catherine.

It was a small apartment house, one tenant to a floor, and there was nobody to open the door of the car. "I don't see why Gavin lives in such a dump," grumbled Miss Garrett. "He doesn't have to. Get out first and keep my skirt off the running-board."

Catherine obeyed. Miss Garrett settled the collar of her ermine coat more becomingly around her neck, and assumed the famous smile. When she had descended, Catherine closed the door of the car, and hung behind so that she would not spoil the pictures. All the photographers tried to crowd in front of the star simultaneously.

"Walk slowly," said one. "Give us a chance." Another was crying: "Look at me, Miss Garrett. Look at me!"

She smiled, the bulbs flashed; they made way for her, and she entered the building.

The entrance door led directly into a small, square foyer with a single elevator. The operator was a sharp-featured young white man with an insinuating smile. As soon as he had closed the elevator door he turned around, saying:

"Good evening, Miss Garrett. Hope it's not a liberty but I seen you in your play on Thursday night. It was swell!"

Gail smiled automatically. "Thank you."

"He had a nerve!" muttered Catherine when they stepped from the elevator.

"I am the servant of the public," murmured Gail plaintively.

The door of the apartment was opened not by Gavin's Hillman, but a man engaged for the evening. From the foyer double glass doors led into a sunroom which was filled with growing plants and had a little fountain playing in the middle. It was the penthouse which had attracted Gavin to the otherwise undistinguished apartment house on Madison Avenue. He had leased it while the building was still going up, and had designed the big sunroom after his own ideas. One side of it, filled with glass, made an immense bow jutting into the roof garden. Gavin was in the sunroom now mixing a cocktail at a portable bar. Gail waved her hand to him and turned aside in the corridor leading to the bedrooms.

"You needn't trouble to show me," she said to the servant. "I know the way."

In the guest-room Catherine took her mistress' cape, and handed her what she required from the little dressing-case the maid carried. Gail studied herself in the mirror with the anxiety of a beauty of forty-three. Her figure was still willowy, but after forty, blonde hair, no matter what you do to it, is apt to betray. She was wearing a virginal dress of white chiffon with puffs shirred at the shoulders, and a skirt shirred in tiers. The tense look in her eyes displeased her.

"Eye-drops," she said, and Catherine got out the bottle and the dropper.

"How do I look?" asked Gail when this operation was finished.

"Lovely, Miss," said Catherine. "White suits you so well!"

"That's what you always say," said Gail, "whether I am wearing black or red or green."

Catherine primmed her lips a little. It was as if she had said, "Then why ask?"

"You may go now," said Gail. "Tell Martin I shan't want him again tonight. I'll taxi home."

"Is it safe?" murmured Catherine.

"Oh, somebody will bring me."

When she entered the sunroom Gavin came to meet her. He was frankly forty-five and handsomer than he had ever been; the lines in his face were lines of distinction. "Lovely!" he murmured, picking up her hand and conveying it to his lips.

Gail's smile became tight. "Only my hand?" she said.

"The servant is still in sight."

She looked over her shoulder. "He's gone now."

He pressed her lips lightly with his own.

A flicker of anger crossed Gail's face. "It wasn't always like that," she said.

"I didn't want to rumple you, my dear."

"Ah, don't make pretences! I can see through you perfectly!"

"Cigarette?" he said, offering the box.

"No!" She immediately changed her mind and helped herself. She turned away, and glancing in a mirror, tried to smooth her face out. "You can't make me quarrel with you," she said.

"I'm not trying to."

He was smiling broadly, and that angered her afresh. She struggled with it. "How about the new play? Is it finished?"

"All but," he said. "In another week."

"Tell me about it."

"My dear," he protested, "you know I never talk about my work. Wasn't it Stevenson who said you must never show unfinished work to anybody?"

"That's not what Stevenson said. He said never show unfinished work to women or fools."

"Well, I never show it to anybody."

"So you say. Mack Townley has announced that he is going to produce the play in January."

"That's the usual press stuff. Mack knows no more about the play than its title, 'The Changeling.'"

"Do you mean to say he is willing to produce it sight unseen?"

"Well, after we have been working together for eighteen years, that's not very strange. . . . Cocktail?"

"No, thank you."

"I have got to the age where I need it."

"This talk of your growing old is all nonsense," said Gail angrily. "It doesn't fool me."

"You're wrong," said Gavin, holding his glass up to the light. "It's the cause of the misunderstanding between us. I am getting old."

She bit her lip. "Well, never mind that . . . Am I to have the leading part in the new play?"

"Ah, let's don't talk business," said Gavin, cajolingly.

"I insist on an answer! That's why I came early. You never give me a chance to see you alone. I have to make my plans as well as Mack Townley."

"There is no part in it worthy of you," said Gavin. "It's a man's play."

"There must be a woman in it, or it wouldn't be your play."

"The only important woman's part is that of a young girl."

Gail flung her cigarette violently on the floor. "I thought so! I thought so!" she cried. "Why don't you say right out that I'm too old to act in your plays!"

"Gail, for God's sake!" he remonstrated.

She looked more than her age now. The repulsion that she could see in his eyes made her worse. "So this is what I get for having given the best years of my life! For having devoted all my art to making you famous! You owe your fame to me! To me! Do you hear? Where would you have been if I had not breathed life into the silly puppets in your plays?"

Gavin's face hardened. "You are a great actress," he said. "I have never failed to acknowledge my debt to you. . . . But just now you are making a show of yourself."

"How dare you!" she gasped. "O God! that I should live to hear a man speak to me like that! That I should be discarded for an ingénue! I won't bear it! I won't . . . !"

He seized her wrist to make her listen to him. "There are strange servants in the flat," he said. "Do you want to read all this in the gossip columns tomorrow?"

"I don't care! I don't care!" she cried; nevertheless she lowered her voice. The husky tones were venomous. "I'm not going to take this from you! I'm not the sort of woman who can be chucked aside like an old hat. I'll show you up. I'll ruin you! O God! How I hate you! Smug and sneering as you are . . ."

Gavin put in mildly: "I never sneered at anybody in my life."

"You lie! You're sneering now! I could kill you for the way you've used me! I could kill you . . . !"

A bell sounded in the distance. Gail caught her breath on a gasp, and running out, turned towards the guest-room at the end of the corridor. She passed the manservant on his way to the entrance door. Gavin poured another cocktail.

CHAPTER TWO

EMMETT GUNDY, the novelist, and his friend, Louella Kip, were on their way to Gavin Dordress' apartment in a taxicab. Emmett was bundled up in a blue rumble-seat coat belted around the waist, the only one of that color in New York, he claimed. With the collar turned up and his hat brim snapped down in front, all that could be seen of him were his glittering dark eyes, and small, carefully trained mustache. Louella was one of the army of free-lance writers who somehow manage to scrape a living without ever becoming known to the public. A little faded woman with a harassed expression, she looked twenty years older than Emmett, but they were in fact the same age. Emmett looked her over critically.

"That dress has seen better days," he remarked.

"Well, you know the state of my wardrobe," said Louella philosophically. "It's the best I have. Mr. Dordress is a friendly man. He won't care."

"There will be others present."

"If you are ashamed of my appearance you shouldn't have brought me," said Louella, plucking up spirit.

"Gavin invited you. I merely conveyed the invitation."

"Were you hoping I would decline?" she asked quietly.

He did not answer her. "Gavin will be friendly enough if you flatter him," he said bitterly. "He doesn't care who it comes from."

"He doesn't need flattery," said Louella. "He's at the top of his profession."

"You would say that. Just to be disagreeable. You mean that he makes more money than any other playwright of the day. Money isn't everything. As a matter of fact, Gavin Dordress hasn't a spark of original talent. What he has is a talent for publicity. He understands the politics of the theater. He knows what wires to pull. It is Gail Garrett and Mack Townley who have made him."

"Everybody else says that it was Gavin Dordress who made them."

"Oh, I dare say! Nothing succeeds like success. He's got you going like all the other women. Gavin has made his way step by step through using women. A male charmer, that's what he is."

"How can you say such a thing?" she murmured.

"But he can't fool me," Emmett went on. "I've known him too long. I've known him since he was a half-baked frosh in college."

"You were a freshman, too, then."

"Sure; but I made good. I was famous before I graduated from college. My first book sold forty thousand copies. It was four or five years after that before Gavin even got a production. His first play was a complete flop."

"I hate to hear you talk about him like that," murmured Louella. "Your oldest friend!"

"Sure he's my friend. So what?"

"It sounds as if you hated him."

"Don't be silly. I see him as he is, that's all. He can't pull any wool over my eyes." Emmett laughed bitterly. "I've got to hand it to Gavin for his cleverness. I only wish I could get away with it. It doesn't pay to be sincere. Tripe is what they want, and tripe is what they pay for!"

This started Louella's thoughts in a new direction. "What did Middlebrook say about your novel?" she asked.

"He was keen to publish it," said Emmett, "but I told him to go to hell."

"Why?" she asked blankly.

"Because he suggested certain changes that showed he completely misunderstood it. I took the script and walked out."

"Oh, Emmett!"

"Well, do you expect me to prostitute myself to an ignorant fool like Middlebrook? He's a butcher, not a publisher. He buys and sells novels by the pound—like the tripe they are!"

"What will you do?" she murmured. "What will we both do?"

"Have you been turned down, too?" he asked sharply. "Your articles for the *Metropolitan*?"

"No," she said sadly. "I give them what they want. I have no talent, so it doesn't matter. But they have reduced my rate. There are so many younger writers in the field."

"Middlebrook is not the only publisher," growled Emmett. "But the novel has been turned down so many times!"

"Gavin could help me if he wanted to," said Emmett sorely. "With a recommendation from him any publisher would bring it out."

"Have you asked him?"

"Sure! He's read the script."

"What did he say?"

"He intimated that he didn't think much of it. Oh, very delicately, of course. Suggested that I try something else. Pure professional jealousy. He is enough of a writing-man to recognize real talent when he sees it. You can hardly blame him. Said that novels were a bit out of his line, and offered me a hundred to tide me over."

"Another hundred?"

"Well, why not? What's a lousy hundred to Gavin? He makes a hundred thousand a year."

"But it mounts up so. How will you ever pay him back?"

"That's the least of my troubles."

"Emmett," she said earnestly, "let's start in on your script tomorrow and go over it chapter by chapter . . ."

"So you think I can no longer write," he said harshly. "You, too!"

"No, Emmett, no! I believe in you. I shall always believe in you."

"You think you can teach me how to write!"

"No! I have no talent. I have never had any illusions about that. But I've been through a hard school. I know what the public wants.

At least I know what *they say* the public wants. If we could just fix this novel up so you could get an advance on it, you could bring it out under another name if you were ashamed of it."

"That would be artistic suicide."

"But you must live! Gavin Dordress will get tired of lending you money. It's only human nature."

"Is that a way of saying that *you're* getting tired of helping me out?"

Louella lowered her head. "Emmett, how can you say such things to me? After all these years!"

"Oh, for God's sake, don't get emotional!" he said. "We're almost there!"

After a silence Louella said, very low: "I suppose you look on me as a drag on you now. If I were strong enough I ought to leave you."

"So you're talking about deserting me now," he said. "I thought we were leading up to that."

She put her hand over his briefly. "Don't be afraid. I'll never leave you . . . unless you wish me to."

The car stopped. "Press photographers?" she said uneasily.

Emmett turned down the collar of his coat. "Gavin Dordress doesn't often entertain," he said. "Naturally it has news value."

"How did they know about it?"

"Well, I tipped them off, if you must know. Won't do me any harm to be shot as a guest of the great man. . . . You go in first. It's me they want."

CHAPTER THREE

SIEBERT ACKROYD and Cynthia Dordress were driving up the Avenue from Washington Square in Siebert's little convertible with the top down. It was a typical November night, cold, with sparkling stars. Cynthia was enveloped in a beaver coat, Gavin's gift, and had a chiffon veil around her trim head to keep her hair in place. When her hair was covered, it emphasized the clean, pure line of her profile. Siebert was a big young man with strongly marked features and a look of resolution that verged on impatience. Most men, seeing the look in his eye, addressed him politely.

"What a night!" he said. "I wish we could drive right through until morning, without having to go to that silly party at your dad's."

"Dad's parties are not silly," said Cynthia.

"By morning we could be in Virginia," murmured Siebert. "You are sweet enough to eat."

"Long before morning we should be quarreling." said Cynthia.

"Well, is it my fault that we always seem to get in a quarrel?"

"Is it mine?" countered Cynthia.

"Let's not start anything now," said Siebert quickly. "Let me put the case to you in a matter-of-fact way without any heat or passion. I am horribly in love with you. I have gone all out. To be beside you like this is heaven for me. Does that make you sore?"

"Of course not," she said in a softened voice.

"You have me to make or break," he went on. "You come between me and everything. Naturally, such a state of suspense is hell on earth. I am good for nothing."

16

"Now you're beginning to quarrel."

"No! No!" he said quickly. "I am perfectly cool and reasonable. I'm trying to get to the bottom of this. I'm head over heels in love with you, and you surely must love me a little! Why don't we get married?"

"I've told you so many times . . ."

"Yes, but always with anger and insults. Consequently it wasn't convincing. Let's talk it over calmly. We could afford to get married. My agency is only a small affair, but it's solidly founded because I only accept authors for my clients who have something in them, and I do so well for them they will never leave me. Year by year it is bound to pay better. O God! to think of having a home! To come home to you at night . . ."

"You forget that I have my job, too, at the clinic."

"I admit I am jealous of your job," said Siebert. "You are not hard-boiled enough to deal with sick people all day. It takes too much out of you."

"I have the feeling of being useful," said Cynthia, "There is nothing to beat it."

"I wouldn't mind if you worked at home. You should write like your father, and let me be your agent."

"I have no talent for writing."

"Well, I concede the job at the clinic," he said. "We can afford a good servant. Don't you want a home, too? Wouldn't it be lovely to meet in our own home after work and be together until we went to work again?"

"Yes," said Cynthia a little faintly; "but . . ."

"Cyn, for God's sake, if we love each other, why go behind it?"

"You're such a boy!" she murmured.

"Is that where I fall short?"

"Yes. I see through you too clearly. You're no wiser than I am. You never surprise me."

"Well, I'm damned!" he muttered. And after a silence, grimly: "I could surprise you all right if I didn't love you so damned much!"

"I shall never marry," said Cynthia, "unless some man wants me who I feel is bigger and cleverer than myself, and who has reserves that I cannot enter into."

"In other words, a Gavin Dordress," he said with extreme bitterness.

"Now you're just being hateful."

"This feeling for your father is ridiculous!"

"It's not ridiculous; it's only unusual. The circumstances are unusual. It's just a year ago since I saw my father for the first time. My mother was a foolish, light-headed woman. She was jealous of his popularity and his fame. Soon after I was born she divorced him, and regretted it as long as she lived. She kept me away from him, and he made no effort to see me because, as he has told me since, he thought the most important thing was not to come between a child and its mother. Her bitterness against him was pathological, and naturally I absorbed it. I grew up thinking of him as a kind of monster.

"When I did go to see him after my mother's death, it was not with any idea of finding a father; I simply meant to use him as a means of getting on in the world. And then when I saw him and talked to him. . . . Oh, Siebert! I thought I was hiding my hatred and bitterness, but of course he instantly saw it, though he made believe not to. He was so funny and human and casual; so *honest!* Not like a father at all, but somebody my own age. I felt a sympathy and understanding such as I had never known in my mother. Yet he didn't make any effort to win me over, but just let me alone. All my defences went down immediately. I felt as if it would take the rest of my life to make up for the way I misjudged him. During the past year I have seen him almost every day, and my admiration has grown with every meeting. He has never let me down."

"Well, that's all right," said Siebert grudgingly. "Gavin's a right guy. He's your father. He doesn't conflict with me. I am to be your husband." He laughed, not very mirthfully. "A fellow is heavily handicapped in marrying the daughter of such a superman, but I'll chance it."

Cynthia did not respond to the laugh. "You don't understand," she said. "During the past year my father has given me an ideal that I—well, I couldn't take anything less than my ideal, could I?"

Siebert glanced at her in dismay. "Cynthia!"

"You asked for the plain truth," she cried, "and there it is!"

"Damn Gavin Dordress!" he said savagely.

"I hate you when you talk like that!" said Cynthia, seething. "You are merely coarse and shallow! You understand nothing!"

"*Damn* him!" said Siebert. "I hate him!"

Cynthia was near tears then. "You knew him before I came on the scene. It was at his place that I first met you. You were his friend."

"Sure I was his friend. But if anybody hurts me I'm going to strike back!"

They drove up in front of Gavin's house. "I suppose we've got to sit through this damn dinner," Siebert growled.

"I'll see that you're not placed beside me," said Cynthia.

"Go on in," he said. "I'll find a parking-place and follow."

The bulbs flashed as Miss Dordress crossed the sidewalk. "Hold your head up!" yelled the photographers, but she only pressed it lower. When Siebert followed, a few minutes later, one said, "Wipe off that scowl, brother."

"Go to hell," said Siebert.

The bulbs flashed, anyhow.

"Miss Dordress' escort," said a voice. "What's the name, please?"

"Julius Cæsar," said Siebert.

CHAPTER FOUR

THOUGH HE WAS NOT A TALL MAN and far from slender, Amos Lee Mappin stepped out with a good stride, and little Fanny Parran, clinging to his arm, was obliged almost to trot to keep up. Fanny's littleness, her dimples, her blonde curls, and her lisp gave her the artless charm of a child, but a man who assumed to talk baby talk to her was apt to get a shock.

She said: "On the level, Pop, you didn't wangle this invitation for me, did you? Was it Mr. Dordress' very own idea to ask me?"

"Absolutely," said Lee. "He said to me: 'Lee, I'm short a female for Sunday night. Do you think that cheeky little secretary of yours would condescend to accept an invitation?'"

"Go on, Pop!" said Fanny. "Mr. Dordress never said that. He is too dignified."

"You don't know the half of it, my child. Of course I couldn't swear to his exact words, but that was the sense of it."

"Oh, dear!" said Fanny after a moment. "I suppose he *does* think I'm pretty fresh."

"Well, he's considered a good judge of human nature."

"I didn't tell you what happened that day he came to your office, Pop. I was ashamed."

"Good God! Did you assault the man?"

"Don't try to be funny! . . . You see, the Police Commissioner was with you, and Mr. Dordress had to wait a few minutes in the outer room. He looked at me in such a friendly way, I mean as if I was a human being and not just a piece of office furniture, and we got to talking. I can't tell you just how it came about. I was fussed, you see, at being noticed by the great man, and I heard myself saying, 'Mr. Dordress, I think the women in your plays are terrible!'"

Lee chuckled. "Not a bad opening. And what did Gavin say?"

"He said, 'I think so, too!'"

Lee laughed aloud. "It is undoubtedly to that that you owe your invitation to dinner. Gavin is fed up with women who throw fits over him. Strange as it may seem, he's a modest man."

"How kind of him to ask little me!" said Fanny. . . . "Do I look all right, Pop? I won't disgrace you?"

"You do, and you will not," said Lee calmly. "You know that very well already, so stop insulting my intelligence."

"Some men wouldn't force me to fish for compliments," said Fanny.

"I'm your boss, not your boy friend."

"Who will be there besides us?"

"I gather it's a kind of class reunion: Yale '13. Mack Townley and his new wife . . ."

"That's Beatrice Ellerman. She's beautiful."

"Hm!" said Lee.

"Don't you like her, Pop?"

"A man never likes the young wives of his old friends. I think she's taking Mack for a ride."

"But surely with his experience he ought to know what he's doing. After all the beautiful actresses he has hired and fired in his productions."

"That's just it. Over-confidence. Mack thinks he knows the sex. A man can't have his guard up all the time. She watched him until he lowered it, and pinked him! No man is safe."

"You have escaped."

"That's because I know my own weakness. I never try conclusions with a woman. I run away."

"Have you never been in love?"

"Never! I would as soon toy with a cobra!"

"I think you're lying! . . . Who else will be there?"

"Emmett Gundy."

"Who's he?"

"Another one of our classmates. He writes novels. At least, I suppose he still does. I haven't seen anything from his pen lately. In college Emmett was considered the brightest of the lot. But he seems to have flashed in the pan."

"Who is asked for him?"

"I don't know. Years ago Emmett had a girl called Louella Kip. Sweet little thing, and absolutely devoted to him. I have forgotten whether he married her. Gavin keeps up with him."

"Were you all special friends in college?"

"Yes, pretty close. But in a little gang like that there are always fellows who pair off. Gavin and I were the closest. We had been to prep school together. Great days! Seems like yesterday. How well I remember when we discovered the Phoenician alphabet in an old book. For years we used to correspond in it."

"Your class was quite a distinguished one," said Fanny, "what with Gavin Dordress and Mr. Townley and this novelist, whoever he is."

"Gavin Dordress is the only real star we produced."

"Oh, I don't know, Pop; you're not so dusty. Of course you haven't an immense popular following like Gavin Dordress, because you're a specialist. But you're known; your books sell. You're at the head of your specialty."

"Crime, eh?"

"I love it!" said Fanny. "How did you come to adopt crime, Pop?"

"I suppose it's because I'm such a mild man. . . . And of course Gavin's daughter and her young man will be there," he went on.

"He's cute," said Fanny.

"Quite!" said Lee. "Six foot two of cuteness!"

"And what lady will Mr. Dordress ask for himself?"

"Oh, Gail Garrett, of course."

"Why 'of course'? Is that still going on?"

"I don't understand you."

"All right, Prune. . . . Gosh! Think of being asked to dinner with Gail Garrett! I shall be perfectly overwhelmed!"

"Then we will see a phenomenon!"

"That's not very clever. . . . You don't know me, Pop. I mean to be perfectly quiet tonight and take everything in."

"Impossible!"

"What's Gail Garrett like, close to?"

"How am I to answer that? A popular star for twenty-five years. She's not like a mere woman; she's a Broadway institution."

"She must be human."

"Oh, quite!" said Lee, dryly, "in the wrong way. . . . She won't cotton to you."

"Why not? Everybody likes me—or almost everybody."

"Because you have twenty years' advantage of her, that's why."

"I see. Well, I'll try not to provoke her."

As Lee and Fanny approached the steps of the apartment house where Gavin Dordress lived, a photographer said: "Are you going to Mr. Dordress'?"

"Such was our intention," said Lee in his mild manner. "But if Dordress is unfair to labor we'll eat elsewhere."

The photographers grinned and set off their flashes.

"What name, please?"

"Amos Lee Mappin."

"Oh, the detective!"

"Nothing of the sort," said Lee. Fanny was delighted to see Pop getting a little of his own back. "If you must hang a label on me, make it 'amateur criminologist.'"

"Amateur nothing," said the young man, making a note; "famous criminologist. . . . And the young lady?"

"Miss Frances Parran. . . . You can add that I am the author of *The Fine Art of Murder*, on sale at all bookstores."

"The heck with it!" said the young man. "You're the guy that the police consulted in respect to the washtub murder. You solved it for them. That's your news value."

"Well, just as you like," said Lee. He and Fanny entered the apartment house.

CHAPTER FIVE

BEA ELLERMAN, now officially, Mrs. Mack Townley, was one of the most beautiful women in the public eye, and the little cushions of self-satisfaction at the corners of her adorable lips suggested that she knew it. Her tall figure, her classic features, her soft dark hair, all were perfect, and she had, in addition, that all-over lusciousness of aspect that defies description. Her husband could deny her nothing. She was wearing a Hattie Carnegie dress of stiff blue silk besprinkled with tiny gold stars and a fifty-thousand-dollar sable coat; clips, necklace and bracelet of diamonds and emeralds. She sat a little forward in the taxi, smoothing the wrinkles out of her gloves, while Mack, from his corner, watched her with a kind of agony of desire and frustration. A tall man, Mack, beginning to grow a little heavy; dark, handsome, self-indulgent face; famous for his perfect grooming.

"We're half an hour late," he growled.

"What of it?" said Bea. "They won't sit down without us."

"It's damn bad manners!"

"Nonsense! Nobody's on time. Not important people, anyhow. I aimed to be late tonight."

"Why, for God's sake?"

"Because I wasn't going to let Gail Garrett make an entrance on me. That old woman!"

"All right," growled Mack. "But please remember that she's still an important person in my business."

"She's slipping fast. It's ridiculous the way she tries to hang on to Gavin Dordress. Anybody can see that he is sick of her."

"What is it to you?"

"Nothing. But I hate to see Gavin made a fool of."

"Leave it to him."

"A man is no match for a woman in a situation like this. Gavin needs the help of another woman in getting rid of Gail Garrett."

A spasm of anger crossed Mack's face. "Meaning yourself?"

Bea smiled confidently.

"You keep out of this!" growled Mack. "I won't have it!"

Bea leaned over and slid the glass across so that the chauffeur could not hear. "Don't speak to me like that," she said coldly. "I am not accustomed to it."

"All right," said Mack. "But you leave Garrett alone, that's all."

"So she's important to you," said Bea with a disagreeable smile. "Are you thinking of engaging her?"

"No. But I don't want any feud started."

"Mercy! I'm not going to *do* anything. I don't have to. The woman already hates me as much as it is possible for one woman to hate another."

"All right," growled Mack.

Bea smoothed her gloves. "I'm quite looking forward to this dinner," she murmured. "I expect to enjoy myself. I suppose Gavin will put Garrett at his right hand and me at his left. Then we'll see."

Mack drew his lips back. "All right! But don't forget that a man can stand only so much!"

"What on earth are you talking about?" she said, turning to him.

He refused to answer her.

"Are you going to carry on like this every time a man acts as if he liked me?"

"I don't care about any other man. It's only this one man . . ."

"He's your oldest friend."

"So much the worse."

Bea shrugged elaborately. "I don't see how I can act any differently. I certainly can't set out to keep Gavin Dordress at arm's-length. He's your partner. He's absolutely essential to you."

Mack said nothing.

"I should think you'd be glad to help him get rid of an incubus like Garrett. It would be tragic if he gave her the lead in his new play. She's finished. Worse than tragic, it would be bad for business."

"I never interfere with the casting of a Dordress play."

"Don't be a fool!" said Bea sharply. "Let us face realities. Do I or do I not get this part?"

"Better wait and see the play."

"That's got nothing to do with it. There has to be a leading woman's part and I'm going to play it. It's the next step in my career. I've been planning this for years."

"Was that why you married me?" growled Mack.

"For Heaven's sake, this is business!" she said. "Try to look at it from my point of view. The new Dordress play will be the number-one event of the season. Naturally I play the lead. If the play was produced by Mack Townley and Mack Townley's wife did not get the lead, it would be like a slap in the face, it would be like repudiation."

"The final choice rests with Gavin," said Mack.

"Oh, I'll take care of him," said Bea confidently. "I'll see that he wants me to play the part."

Mack's face turned blackish and his right hand clenched instinctively. "By God!" he muttered. "By God! . . ."

Bea, busy with her thoughts, did not notice him. "His giving a dinner at this time falls just right," she said. "I'll get him to tell me about the play. I'll clinch the matter tonight . . ."

Mack broke out in a low, thick voice. "God damn the play! And Gavin Dordress, too! I'll have nothing to do with it. Let him find another manager!"

Bea turned her head swiftly and looked at him from between narrowed lids.

"I'm fed up!" stormed Mack. "Fed up, do you hear? Gavin this and Gavin that; you din his name into my ears from morning until night. The man has laid a spell on you. Do you expect me to stand for it? Gavin and Gavin's play! No, by God! I'm through with him and I'll tell him so tonight. I'm going to take you away from all this!"

"You don't mean what you're saying," put in Bea quietly.

"All right! You'll see!" he cried.

"Listen to me," she said. "You're at the head of your profession in New York and London. But if you drop Gavin Dordress, you will be handing a great fortune to one of your rivals, while you drop into second place!"

"I'm going to retire," muttered Mack. "I've made money enough. We'll travel abroad."

"Who, me?" said Bea. She laughed delicately, and paused to allow the sound to sink in. "Can you see me fluffing from one European resort to another with nothing to do but exchange gossip with the other exiles, and get fat? You can do it if you want. Not me! I'm twenty-nine years old and I'm not going to stop until I get to the top of the ladder. Get that. When I agreed to marry you it was understood that you were to help me in my career. If you chuck your part of the bargain, don't expect me to keep mine. The day you drop Gavin Dordress I go to Reno!"

"By God! you're a cold-blooded proposition!" muttered Mack.

"That doesn't help any," said Bea pettishly. "Really, Mack, I don't understand you. With all your experience you must know that in our profession business is all mixed up with personal relations. You can't separate them. If, in order to get this part, it is necessary for me to cajole the author, and even appear to make love to him a little, why should you care? You must have been through it a hundred times before."

Mack shook his head heavily. "No. Never before," he said quietly. "Because I'm in love with you, Bea, see? And there's something in a man more powerful than business policy, or making money or getting ahead of others. A man may keep it under for years, he may never have known that it was there, but it breaks out . . . it breaks out. . . ."

Bea appeared to relent a little. She patted his hand, but did not look around. She was intent on her own thoughts.

"Tell me you are not so cold-blooded as you make out!"

"Of course I'm not! I was talking business!"

"Tell me you're just a little fond of me."

"Certainly I am. Or I wouldn't have married you."

"Kiss me, Bea!"

She obediently turned her head. "Don't muss me!" she warned. He kissed her gently, his hand closing hard over hers.

"Ouch! You're hurting my hand."

"Sorry, dear. . . . Let's not go to this dinner," he pleaded. "Honestly, I don't feel up to it!"

"But we must!" she said. "We're there! We can't back out now. . . . Besides, the matter may be decided tonight. If I am not there, Garrett will wangle the part out of him!"

"All right," he said heavily. "But I feel that it is a mistake."

"But, Mack, we understand each other now. If you see me being very nice to Gavin you will know it is only through motives of policy."

"You are not nice to him through motives of policy," he said darkly. "The man excites you. I have eyes."

"I will be extra nice to you after we have left," she said softly.

"All right. But don't goad me too far while we're there." It was like a groan. "Don't goad me!"

When they got out of the cab, Mack hung back in order to give the photographers a fair show at Bea. Bea smiled dazzlingly at each young man in turn.

"Hello, boys! We meet again."

"Couldn't be too often for me, Miss Ellerman," said one.

The bulbs flashed. When Bea passed on they took Mack in turn. When Mack had disappeared into the apartment house one young man said to another, "Townley's showing his age."

CHAPTER SIX

GAVIN DORDRESS and his guests had moved into the studio after dinner. This was a big room occupying the entire westerly end of the penthouse, with windows on three sides looking out on the neat box hedges of the roof garden. The window curtains were drawn back and colored lights were strung in the garden to make a festive effect. At the back of the garden the wall of the adjoining building rose some fifteen feet higher, covered with a lattice over which vines were trained in summer. Indoors, Gavin did not go in for decorative fads: the room was of no period, but merely comfortable, with deep chairs, mellow old rugs, shaded lamps and endless shelves of books. A fire was burning.

The setting was right for a good party, and the company highly ornamental. Gavin, Mack, Emmett, and Siebert were tall, handsome men, and Lee, though his figure was tubby, had a distinctive head; all the women were beautiful women, each in her own style, except poor Louella. Nevertheless it was not a good party; there was no lack of brittle talk and laughter, but it had overtones like thunder on the horizon.

Gavin had become aware of it as soon as they sat down at the table. He could not talk all the time; he was hungry. And as soon as he fell silent, the ladies at his right and left, with a too-perfect courtesy and sweetness, began taking shots at each other. In his mind Gavin consigned them both to the devil. His own clever Cynthia was silent and distrait. He could do little with Louella Kip because she was afraid of him. He addressed himself gratefully to

Fanny Parran, whose sharp answers were delightful. But when he talked to Fanny, both Gail and Bea began to discharge their darts in her direction, and Gavin, for Fanny's own sake, felt obliged to leave the girl alone. He was relieved when the ladies left the table.

The men were no better. Mack Townley had drunk too much; Siebert Ackroyd's comely young face was white and tight-lipped. Neither would talk; they glanced at Gavin with barely concealed animosity. Gavin inwardly shrugged them off. In the brightly lighted room Emmett Gundy had the look of a handsome boy who had started to wither before he was quite mature. His would-be flattering remarks were curdled with envy. Nursing his brandy goblet between his hands and sniffing the old Armagnac, he simpered, "This is the incense of popular success." When he lit a cigar he said, "I suppose some Cuban admirer presented you with these."

Only Lee Mappin was his own dry, comical self, and Gavin's heart warmed to him. His best friend! They talked about college days, hoping to draw in the other two classmates, but without success. As soon as the men had drunk their brandies, Gavin led them to the ladies in the sunroom, hoping for the best. The tight smiles which greeted them were not reassuring. What a party! Gavin glanced at Cynthia for humorous sympathy, but Cynthia was sunk in her own painful thoughts. From the sunroom they proceeded to the studio.

Bea Townley, tall, dark, regal in the starry blue dress, looked around. "So this is where masterpieces are produced!"

Gavin said: "I wish I could think so."

"Oh, is this the first time you have been in this room, darling?" asked Gail. Alongside Bea she looked a little insipid. The gathered chiffon dress was too youthful.

Gail was straightening a picture on the wall, and returning a book to its place on the shelf with a proprietary air that made Bea's eyes snap. "Oh dear, no!" said Bea. "I have spent happy hours here. But every time I enter I have the same feeling of awe."

"It will wear off," said Gail.

"Can I have a Scotch and soda?" growled Mack.

"Surely," said Gavin, pressing a bell.

Even the perfect Hillman was upset tonight, Gavin observed with wry humor, when his servant entered, wheeling the bar. Hillman's lean face was drawn and grey; eyes and hands shook a little when he put ice in the glasses.

When Gavin took a glass from him he said: "You may go home with the others when they finish up. If we want anything we'll serve ourselves."

"Yes, sir. Thank you, sir," said Hillman.

After he had left the room Lee Mappin said, just to be saying something: "Doesn't Hillman sleep in?"

"No," said Gavin. "He's a family man. He has a home of his own. Servants ought to be allowed to live normal lives like anybody else."

"Oh!" exclaimed Bea. "Do you mean to say that after the butler goes home you are all alone here on this roof?"

"Surely," said Gavin. "Why not?"

"Aren't you afraid?"

"Hardly. I've reached the age when I love to be alone."

Fanny Parran was beside him at the moment. "That's hardly polite," she murmured.

"Well, do you blame me?" Gavin asked, smiling back.

Fanny glanced over the company. "No. If it was me, I'd tell them all to get the heck out!"

Gavin laughed. "If they were all like you what a good party it would be!"

"You're pretty nice yourself," said Fanny.

Gail and Bea, observing this low-voiced exchange, moved from different directions to break it up. Bea said to Gavin:

"I don't think it's right for you to be alone at night. Suppose you were taken sick!"

"I am never sick," said Gavin. "If I should be, the telephone is beside my bed."

"You might be too sick to use it."

"If I was unconscious, what difference would it make to me?"

"You don't look as if you were going to be sick," said Bea, languishing at him, "but men who are so much in public eye are always a mark for kidnappers, burglars, cranks, and so on."

"Anybody who lives in fear might as well die and be done with it," said Gavin. "The elevator man is there to protect me from intruders. And up here on the fifteenth floor it is hardly likely anybody is coming in by the window."

Gail glanced scornfully at Bea: "Anybody who tried to tackle Gavin would regret it. He is armed."

"Are you?" said Bea.

Gail moved toward an immense flat-topped desk at the south end of the room. She said: "He keeps a gun here." Pulling out the middle drawer, she picked up a business-like black automatic and exhibited it. There was something terrible in her smile.

"You seem to be familiar with them," said Bea.

"I use a gun like this in my present play."

"Put it away, Gail," said Gavin good-humoredly. "I hate to see anybody fooling with a loaded gun."

Bea, her face sharpened by curiosity, had joined Gail at the desk. Gail returned the gun to its place. Bea's eyes ran over the contents of the wide, shallow drawer. Alongside the gun lay a pile of typescript with corrections and interlineations in a quaint and individual hand. At the top of the first page was typed the title, "The Changeling."

"Oh, here is the great play!" cried Bea. "Won't you read it to us, Gavin?"

Gail stood a little away from the desk, watching Bea with a slight, malicious smile. Fanny Parran and Louella Kip, who did not know Gavin very well, added their voices to Bea's.

"Oh do read it, Mr. Dordress!"

Gavin shook his head. "I never read my own stuff aloud," he said, obstinately good-humored.

"Please!" chorused the three women.

Emmett spoke up: "Leave him alone," he said with a sour smile. "He hates to be the center of attraction."

"The truth is," said Gavin, smiling, "I have listened to too many young playwrights laughing and sobbing over their own lines."

"But among your intimate friends . ." pleaded Bea.

"Shut the drawer, Bea," growled Mac. "Can't you see that he hates to have his work touched?"

Bea smiled at her husband in a manner that presaged trouble later, and slowly pushed the drawer in. Returning to Gavin, she said:

"Well, tell us something about the play: tell us the story of it."

"Not a word," said Gavin, smiling and firm. "It's the only rule I ever made for myself—and kept."

"Then nobody in the world but you knows what is in that play?" said Bea.

"Nobody in the world! . . . Mack is taking a big chance in announcing its production."

"I could still refuse to produce it," growled Mack.

Everybody except Gavin laughed as at a good joke. Bea, laughing the loudest, said to Mack: "You won't do that!"

"Oh, I don't know," he growled.

Gavin glanced at him, puzzled. Mack refused to meet his eye.

It was Emmett Gundy who made the first move to break up the ill-starred party. He exchanged a meaning look with Louella and they arose.

It was no more than ten o'clock. The inevitable empty politenesses were exchanged.

"Must you go? It's so early."

"Sorry," said Emmett, "but we have promised to join some friends at the Coq Rouge."

Louella looked as if this was news to her. She had too honest a face for society. Gavin and Cynthia accompanied them to the door of the room.

"Are you going to be tied up tomorrow, Gavin?" asked Emmett offhandedly.

"I'll be working on my play, I haven't made any engagements."

"Could I see you for a few minutes after working-hours? I want to ask your advice about rewriting my novel."

"Surely. Drop in about five."

When they had gone, Gavin said, low-voiced: "Stand by me, Cyn. I want you to stay until after everybody has gone."

She looked quickly in his face. "Surely, Dad."

Lee and Fanny were on their feet. "Must you go?" said Gavin with real regret.

"Must!" said Lee. They moved into the foyer and he added: "Fanny and I thought this would be the quickest way to break it up. This party was doomed not to prosper."

"Dear old Lee!" said Gavin warmly.

"Why this sudden burst of affection?"

"You shine like a good deed in a naughty world!"

"I've been called many things in my time," said Lee. "But that's a new one."

"I'm sorry it wasn't a good party," said Gavin to Fanny.

"Ask me again."

"I shall."

When Gavin and Cynthia turned to go back, they met Siebert, very stiff and good-looking, coming out of the studio. Cynthia with the slightest of bows passed on into the room.

"Must you go?" said Gavin. "I was hoping you would stay."

"Thanks," said Siebert, "but I'm sure you and Cynthia want a little time together."

Gavin was drawn to this young man. "It's a long time since you have dropped in on me, Siebert. When are we going to have another game of chess?"

"Chess is all very well for you," said Siebert, "but I have my way to make. I can't take the time for it."

"Well . . . I'm sorry," said Gavin. "You had the makings of a good player. Good-night, Siebert."

Siebert went on to get his things.

Gavin looked weary when he reentered the studio. In the beginning he had exerted himself to make things go; now he didn't care. Thus, when Mack growled, "Get your things, Bea," he said nothing.

Bea made no move. "It's only ten o'clock," she said. "Gavin will think we're not enjoying ourselves. Sit here, Gavin."

Gavin sat beside her. Mack left the room. Bea looked after him indifferently, and rattled on:

"You and Cynthia must dine with us very soon, and that handsome fellow, Siebert . . . and of course you, Gail."

"Thanks," said Gail.

She was sitting opposite them with a ghastly fixed smile. She was squeezing a handkerchief in her hand, and she had bitten off all the lip-stick from her lower lip without knowing it. Bea, flaunting her beauty and freshness, said:

"What night shall it be, Gavin? I want to make this a very special occasion."

"I'd rather not make any engagements until I get the play off my hands; four or five days; a week at the outside."

"Very well. I want to consult you about the other guests. . . ."

Bea's flow was checked by the return of Mack. He had her coat over his arm. "Come on," he said. Bea saw that she could not defy him without creating a scene, and got up slowly.

"Husbands are so peremptory!"

All five of them passed out into the foyer, and stood there while Mack helped his wife into her coat. Gail made no move to get her things. "Can we put you down anywhere, Gail, dear?" said Bea.

"Thanks, darling. I'm not quite ready."

Bea's eyes glittered. She glanced across the sunroom. "How lovely the garden looks under the lights!" she said. "Show it to me, Gavin. It won't take a minute."

"Very well," said Gavin woodenly.

They crossed the sunroom. The key to the garden door hung alongside the door-frame. Gavin opened the door and they went out, closing the door behind them. The three waiting in the foyer could see them dimly through the glass. Gavin was calling Bea's attention to something off to the south. Bea slipped her hand cosily under his arm and they passed out of sight.

"I'd like to see the garden, too," Gail said, her voice unnaturally sharp.

She crossed the sunroom and went out, leaving the door open. Outside she started to run. Mack watched her for a moment, glowering, then silently went after her. Cynthia, after hesitating painfully, followed Mack.

They found Gavin and Bea standing beside the parapet at the east end of the roof. Behind them a wasted moon was rising over the river, and the pin-point lights of Queensborough stretched away to infinity. When Cynthia come up to the group, Gail was saying shrilly:

"You better look after your wife, Mack! She needs it!"

"Don't want your help," growled Mack.

"She's loose! She's common! She's cheap!" shrilled Gail. "See her trying to brazen it out . . ."

"Gail, for God's sake, be quiet!" said Gavin. His voice was weary with disgust.

"Come in!" growled Mack to Bea, with a jerk of his head towards the house door.

"You have no right to speak to me like that!" retorted Bea. "Am I your servant?"

Mack raised his voice slightly. "Come in!" he repeated. "Or you'll get worse."

Bea turned to Gavin. "You hear, he threatens me! He's mad! It is dangerous for me to go with him!"

"He is your husband," said Gavin coldly.

Mack made straight for the door of the apartment. He held it open for Bea to pass through. She, having recovered herself partly, took her time about it. "I'm going," she said to Gavin, "not because he orders me to, but because I want to end a painful situation. Good-night, Gavin. Good-night, Cynthia, dear. Good-night, Gail." She went out with a nonchalant air. Gail sneered.

Mack, preparing to follow Bea, looked furiously at Gavin. "Give your play to whoever you like," he said. "I'm through!"

"That suits me," said Gavin levelly. The door slammed.

Gail, with a grotesque attempt to recover her usual sugary manner, said: "Cynthia, darling, I want a few words alone with Gavin. You will excuse us, I'm sure. Such old friends!"

Cynthia looked at her father, then at Gail. She said coolly: "I'm sorry, but Dad just said he wanted to speak privately to me."

Gail caught her breath and looked at Gavin. "Is this true?"

"You heard her," said Gavin.

Gail could scarcely articulate now. "So! So! You put this child ahead of me now! You're using her as a shield! This chit! Don't think that I can't see through your pitiful evasions. . . ."

Cynthia ran away down the corridor. Gail was still storming when she returned with the ermine coat over her arm. "Your coat, Miss Garrett."

"Am I being put out of the house now?" cried Gail.

Her face was so distorted with rage neither Gavin nor Cynthia could bear to look at her. Since she refused to put her arms through the sleeves of her coat, Cynthia hung it over her shoulders. Gavin opened the door.

"Are you going to let me go down into the street alone?" cried Gail. "Me? There is no doorman in this miserable house to find me a taxi!"

Gavin hesitated.

"Hillman is still here," said Cynthia. She ran into the pantry and fetched the butler out.

"Hillman," said Gavin, "go down with Miss Garrett and get her a cab."

"Yes, sir."

"You'll be sorry for this, Gavin!" cried Gail. "Remember, I warned you! . . . I warned you!"

Gavin closed the door, and he and Cynthia looked at each other. "What a mess!" he said wearily. "My child, I'm so sorry you had to be let in for it!"

"It won't hurt me," said Cynthia. "I'm not made of glass." She laughed shakily. "You are too attractive to the ladies, Dad."

"It's not my attractiveness," said Gavin, "but something more sordid. These women are fighting to get a part in my play."

"Which one gets it?"

"Neither."

They dropped on a sofa alongside the fire. After a while Cynthia said:

"I'd better go, too. I feel done up, and so do you."

"Don't go," said Gavin. "Why don't you stay all night?"

"I haven't my things."

"I wish you'd come here and live," he said wistfully. "It would be so jolly to have you in the house."

She shook her head firmly. "I love my independence. And so do you. We can be friends without living together."

"I shall never give another party," said Gavin. "Why do people give parties?"

"Don't say that."

"Even Hillman. What the devil do you suppose is the matter with Hillman?"

"He confided in me a little yesterday," said Cynthia. "He is married to an ambitious wife. She twits him all the time because he's only a servant. She tells him that their children are old enough now to be ashamed of him. She wants him to give up his job and do something for himself. Hillman tells her he has no money. She says if he would use his wits he wouldn't be without money."

"Poor devil!"

Cynthia stood up. "I must go, Dad."

"Wait! What's the trouble between you and Siebert?"

Cynthia turned away her head. "Ah, don't ask me! He's impossible! Always pestering me to marry him!"

"Aren't you a little in love with him?"

She looked at the floor. "Yes," she murmured. "That's just the trouble. He's so good to look at . . . and such a boy! But I can't respect him, Dad!"

"Siebert's a good lad; sound at heart; able, too."

"I know. I know. But he has no imagination, none of the finer qualities."

"What of it? These sensitive, imaginative creatures are not easy to live with, Cyn. Siebert is very much of a man."

"You can say that about him?" she said in surprise. "You ought to hear the way he abuses you!"

Gavin laughed. "Jealous, eh? I seem to be in everybody's way!"

"Don't say that!" cried Cynthia, putting her arms around him. "You are my ideal!"

He kissed her good-night at the door. "We'll feel better in the morning, Cyn."

"Will you go to bed now?" she asked.

"I'll read a little while to compose my mind. I'll call you when I wake."

"Do, dear."

Hillman came out of the pantry. "Shall I get you a cab, Miss?" he asked.

"No, indeed. I am accustomed to going about by myself."

"Good-night, Miss."

"Good-night, Hillman."

In the elevator the boy Joe asked her with a sharp look, "Is the party over, Miss?"

"Yes," she said. "Why do you ask?"

"Well, everybody's in the house now except the real late birds. If I'm not wanted for a couple of hours I could get a sleep."

As Cynthia waited on the corner for a taxi, an odd-looking figure passed by, a tall man with heavy, stooping shoulders, a foreigner by the look of him. An old, yellowish overcoat as shapeless as a bag hung from his shoulders without touching him anywhere, and he wore a leather aviator's helmet that fastened under his chin. He kept his head down as he walked; he had on thick glasses and had an uncanny way of looking around them. At the moment Cynthia scarcely noticed him, but the strangeness of his appearance impressed him on her subconsciousness.

CHAPTER SEVEN

CYNTHIA LIVED in a small walk-up apartment, parlor, bedroom, and bath, in a converted dwelling in West Fifty-fifth Street, not half a mile from Gavin's place. She let herself in and threw her coat on a sofa. Her little living-room no longer seemed the same haven of peace and freedom. One of the first things that caught her eye was a framed photograph of Siebert on her desk. She thrust it face down in a drawer. After a while she drifted back to the desk and, taking out the photograph, looked at it a long time. She glanced at the clock—10:50. After painful hesitation, she picked up the telephone and dialed a number. She decided to give Siebert a chance to say he was sorry.

He did not answer. She hung up and, going slowly into the bedroom, started to undress. For a long time she lay open-eyed in her bed, waiting for the telephone. It did not ring. When she finally slept with wet lashes on her cheeks, her sleep was broken by bad dreams. Distorted faces formed and dissolved in front of her: Gail Garrett; Mack Townley; the envious Emmett Gundy; the sharp-featured elevator boy; even Hillman, weak, desperate, and furtive.

She was awakened by a roaring that seemed to be inside her head. It resolved itself into the ringing of the telephone bell. She glanced at the bedside clock; 7:30. Her face cleared as if by magic, and she ran into the next room with shining eyes.

But it was not the deep voice that she longed to hear, and her face fell. This was a man's voice so distracted and broken she did not recognize it.

40

"Miss Dordress?"

"Yes. Who is it?"

"Hillman, Miss! . . . Oh, Miss! . . . There has been an accident I don't know how to tell you . . . !"

An icy hand was laid on Cynthia's breast. "My father?"

"Yes, Miss. . . . Come quickly!"

"What has happened?" cried Cynthia.

The frantic Hillman had already hung up.

She threw on her clothes anyhow and got a cab at the door. In five minutes she was at the door of the Madison Avenue apartment. Short as the time was, a thousand horrors had suggested themselves. She fought them off by saying to herself: Hillman is a fool! He exaggerates the trouble.

There was a different boy on the elevator. This was Harry, whom Cynthia liked. "What has happened?" she asked him breathlessly. He turned away his head. "I don't know, Miss. They'll tell you." He is afraid to tell me! she thought; it is the worst!

Hillman opened the door of the apartment. His eyes were red-rimmed, his hands shaking. At the sight of her his eyes filled with weak tears. "Oh, Miss . . ."

"What has happened?" cried Cynthia.

"Your father . . ." He was unable to go on.

Cynthia turned to run to her father's bedroom.

"Not there. He's in the studio."

When she turned in that direction, he caught hold of her. "You mustn't go in there."

Cynthia, frozen, dropped weakly in a chair, staring at the man. "Is he? . . . is he? . . . am I too late?"

Hillman nodded. "Mr. Dordress has passed away."

"No! It *can't* be so!"

"Yes, Miss. Many hours ago."

Cynthia covered her face with her hands. She did not weep. "Send for Mr. Mappin," she whispered.

"He's on his way, Miss."

When the bell rang Cynthia turned her haggard face to see who it was. Two or three important-looking men pushed in as if they had a right to enter. One was in uniform with a lot of gold braid. Police! Several underlings followed, carrying paraphernalia of different sorts.

"This way, please, gentlemen," stammered Hillman, leading them towards the studio.

"What are the police doing here?" whispered Cynthia.

When the bell rang again she went to the door herself. It was Lee Mappin. He took her in his arms. "My dear, dear child!"

She drew herself away. "Never mind me. Go in there, Lee. In there! And for God's sake come and tell me what has happened."

She dropped back in the chair and waited like a woman of stone.

When Lee entered the studio he saw the body of his friend lying huddled on the floor near the fireplace. He drew a long breath to steady himself. Gavin's right arm was outstretched, and near it lay a black automatic as if it had been knocked from his hand as he fell. Under his head a pool of blood had spread out on the parquet floor and coagulated. The wound itself was hidden. Gavin's eyes were fixed and staring. Near him a police photographer was kneeling on the floor, preparing to take a picture of the body. Lee looked around the room. The set-up was familiar to him: captain of the precinct; lieutenant of detectives, another detective, medical examiner, fingerprint expert, and soon.

Captain Kelleran knew him. "Good God! Mr. Mappin, what are you doing here!" he exclaimed.

"Gavin Dordress was my oldest friend," said Lee.

"I didn't know that. You have my sympathy."

"When did this happen?" asked Lee.

"About nine hours ago. Say ten-thirty or eleven last night. There is nothing here to interest us professionally. Clearly a suicide."

"He had everything to live for," murmured Lee.

"He left a letter," said the captain, handing Lee a manila sheet that appeared to have been torn off a pad on Gavin's desk. "I take it that's his handwriting?"

Gavin as a young man had taken the trouble to form a highly decorative hand. The quaintly formed characters were inimitable. "Undoubtedly," said Lee. He read the letter with a masklike face.

"Do you recognize the gun?" asked the captain.

Instead of answering directly, Lee went to the desk at the other end of the room and pulled out the middle drawer. He said: "Gavin kept his gun here. It's gone. It was of the same style and caliber as that on the floor. We may assume that that is his gun."

"So you see . . ." said the captain, spreading out his hands. "We'll check fingerprints on the gun to make sure. There are powder burns around the wound."

There was something else about the drawer that made Lee look thoughtful. He returned to the fireplace. The fire had been out for many hours. On top of the dead embers lay the charred remnants of many burned papers. One sheet had partly fallen out, and the top of it was unburned. Lee could read a typed title: "The Changeling." So Gavin had burned the new play before killing himself. This was no business of the policemen's and Lee said nothing about it.

Taking the letter, Lee returned to Cynthia in the foyer. She raised her questioning eyes to his, and he said simply, "Gavin has left us."

"What was it?" she whispered. "Heart? . . . Why the police?"

"He took his own life."

Cynthia, wildly staring, stammered, "No, Lee, no!"

He put a hand on her shoulder. "You must face it, my dear. He had the right to leave us if he wished to."

"Yes," she agreed. "But he *couldn't* have done it. . . . Last night when I left him there was no such thought in his mind. He was looking ahead to our future. . . ."

"Then it was a sudden impulse."

"No, Lee! Dad was not a creature of impulse. He was stable!"

Lee handed her the letter. A spasm of pain crossed the girl's face at sight of the decorative characters. There was neither salutation nor signature. She read:

> "I have reached the summit of my life—indeed I appear to have passed it. I have done my best work. There is nothing before me but a slow decline in power. I wish to be remembered by my best, and so

I choose to write The End while I can do it firmly.
Men live too long.

"This is my last thought: Man is not worthy of
his beautiful earth. The worst that has been said
about man's life is true; it is cruel, ugly, and evil—
but who would give up the privilege of sitting in on
so magnificent a show? I have seen it, and I leave
the theater without regret."

Cynthia's tears were falling fast before she came to the end.
Some moments passed before she could speak. "Was this all?" she
whispered. "Nothing . . . not one word for me?"

"That is all," said Lee.

"He would not leave me without a word!" she cried. "I will not
believe that he killed himself! . . . There are people who wished
him dead."

"It must be faced," said Lee. "There is the gun, the powder
marks. The letter sounds like Gavin."

"It sounds like him," she agreed; "but it has a made-up sound.
It is like something he might have written in a play."

"Cynthia, my dear, you are only tormenting yourself!"

"Why shouldn't I be tormented?" she burst out. "He would not
leave me without a word. . . . Listen, Lee, we came close to each
other for a moment last night as I was leaving. There was nothing
much said. We understood each other without speaking. You cannot mistake such a moment. After that he *could not* have left me
without a word. I do not believe he killed himself. I will never believe it. . . . Look at this letter! Notice how in the first line he has
changed 'apex' to 'summit'; farther on below he wrote 'most men'
and then crossed out 'most'. Would a man be thinking about literary effect when he was about to die?"

"Habit, perhaps," said Lee. "He wrote the letter. How else can
it be explained?"

"It sounds like something out of a play," insisted Cynthia. "Let
us read the new play and see if there is not a clue there."

"He burned it," said Lee.

"Burned it? Why should he?"

"Well, he implies in the letter that he was dissatisfied with it."

"Implies! Implies! Words can imply so many things! He doesn't say that he was dissatisfied with it. He told me he thought is was *good*."

"Sometimes there is a reaction. Every writer knows what that is."

Cynthia was not listening. "Lee, suppose that this letter is something that Dad wrote for his play. He was always making changes and inserting new pages either in type or longhand. The murderer found it. He would then be obliged to destroy the rest of the play, wouldn't he, in order to conceal the fact that this had been taken from it?"

"That is too far-fetched!" objected Lee.

"What do you mean, far-fetched?"

"It is incredible that the murderer—if there was a murderer—should have stumbled on something that came so pat to his needs."

"Perhaps he read the play first and this letter suggested the plan of the murder."

"Gavin would allow no one to read the play."

"There were plenty of people who were crazy to get a line on it. Hillman may have betrayed Dad while he was out. Hillman . . ." She pulled up suddenly, and her eyes widened.

"What is it?" asked Lee.

"Hillman has something on his mind."

"Naturally, after . . ."

"Oh, this began many days ago."

"Where does Hillman live?" asked Lee.

"I don't know. It's in Gavin's address-book."

Captain Kelleran came out of the studio with his men tailing after him. He bowed to Cynthia with grave sympathy and drew Lee aside. "There is nothing in this case for the police," he said. "With an ordinary magnifying-glass we could identify Mr. Dordress' fingerprints on the gun without the necessity of taking photographs. The medical examiner will hand you the necessary permit for burial, and we will trouble you no more. Please convey my sympathy to the young lady."

"Thank you. She will appreciate it, Captain." Lee shepherded them out through the door.

When they were left alone Cynthia came and wound her arms around Lee's neck. "Thank God I have you!" she said.

"Bless your heart!" he murmured.

"Have I convinced you that Gavin did not kill himself?" she asked, looking deep into his eyes.

"No, my dear," he said gravely. "So far this is only a surmise on your part. We must have evidence."

"Then look for it! Look for it!" she said, urging him with her hands. "Before anything is moved or changed, before anyone else comes. You can lay bare the truth, Lee, if anybody can."

"I'll do my best," he said.

CHAPTER EIGHT

THE BELL RANG. "This will be the reporters," said Lee.

"Don't let them in!" exclaimed Cynthia in horror.

Lee stopped Hillman on his way to the door. "Wait a minute." He said to Cynthia: "We can't keep them out, my dear. I'll take care of them. You go into the guest-room. You should stay here for the present, because you can't protect yourself from intruders in your own place. I'll send for Fanny Parran to be with you."

"I don't want anybody."

"Fanny is a woman in a thousand. She'll act as if nothing was the matter."

"I want to be with Dad," said Cynthia piteously.

Lee thought of the black stain under Gavin's head. "You shall be," he promised. "When I get these people out of the house."

Lee took the precaution of locking the studio door and pocketing the key. A swarm of reporters and photographers was then admitted. More were arriving constantly. Lee told them a plain story of what had happened, and let them copy Gavin's letter. He answered every question that he considered a proper one, but nipped in the bud every attempt to make a sensational mystery of the case. That section of the press which thrives on sensation was disappointed. One or two of the men from the more unscrupulous sheets edged to the door of the studio and tried it. Lee said:

"That's all now, boys. I've got a lot to do. I'll receive you again at eleven o'clock to give you anything that may break in time for the later editions."

47

They left.

Fanny arrived, saddened and wondering. Lee said to her: "I rely on you. Keep your ears open and your mouth shut. I want you to stay with Cynthia for the present. Keep her occupied if you can. There must be family letters to write and so on. She is under the delusion that her father was murdered and we must appear to humor it."

Fanny's eyes widened. "You don't think that . . ."

"Please God there's nothing in it!" said Lee. "One can face the fact that Gavin left us because he wished to go, but if he was taken . . . !"

"Read that!" he said, handing her the letter. "What does it suggest to a woman's intuition?"

Fanny read the letter and considered. "It sounds," she said slowly "—what shall I say? just a little hifalutin for a man so simple and natural as Mr. Dordress."

Lee looked at her in surprise. "That's what Cynthia said. I hope you're both wrong. Go to her."

Lee locked himself in the studio for an hour. When he came out his mild face was stern and grey. Meeting Hillman drifting around the foyer like a lost soul, he said:

"You may telephone for the undertaker now. Let him arrange the body suitably on a couch in there, and see that the floor is washed, so that Miss Cynthia may see her father before he is taken away."

Lee went on to the two girls in the guest-room. When Cynthia saw his face she cried out:

"What have you discovered?"

He hesitated.

"Tell me everything that is in your mind," she pleaded. "Treat me like a man. It is the kindest thing you can do. What I cannot bear is to be kept in the dark."

"I agree," said Lee. "What I have discovered raises a doubt in my mind that Gavin killed himself."

"I knew he wouldn't leave me without a word," murmured Cynthia.

"What did you find?" asked Fanny.

Lee still had Gavin's letter in his hand. He said: "The yellow pad from which this sheet was presumably torn was not lying on Gavin's desk when we were in the room last night. The inference is that he got it out later. If you run your finger lightly along the top of this paper you can feel microscopic pieces of glue clinging to it. When I placed this sheet on top of the pad and examined the edges under a strong glass, I saw that these specks of glue do not fit with the glue that remains on the pad. In other words, this is not the last sheet that was torn off that pad. As a matter of fact, the pad was twice as thick as it is at present when this sheet was torn off it."

The eyes of both girls widened when they took in the significance of this.

"Also," Lee went on, "Gavin's fountain pen was on his desk. I find that he uses the sort of fluid that writes blue and darkens with time. When I made tests with the ink I saw at once that this letter was not written last night. It is several days old, possibly more than a week."

"What did I tell you?" said Cynthia.

"Wait! It is possible that Gavin may have written this several days ago and have been keeping it."

Cynthia shook her head. "He could not have had any such idea when he was talking to me last night."

"A forgery?" suggested Fanny.

"We may dismiss that possibility," said Lee. "Gavin certainly wrote this letter."

"For some other purpose," said Cynthia obstinately.

"You may be right, but until we have further evidence we must still reckon on the possibility of suicide. . . . There is something else."

"Yes?" asked Cynthia anxiously.

"Six little marks on Gavin's forehead, as if he had struck against something, not hard. I don't know yet what they signify. The police were so sure it is suicide they paid no attention. I have made a sketch of the marks."

"Anything else?" asked Cynthia.

"I found Gavin's address-book, but the little book bound in green Morocco in which he entered ideas for plots, scenes, and characters is missing."

"It was always in Gavin's desk," said Cynthia.

"What happened last night after Fanny and I went home?" asked Lee.

Cynthia described what had taken place word by word, as closely as she could remember.

Lee said: "I noticed that there was a certain coldness between you and Siebert last night."

She told him briefly what had happened.

There was a knock on the door. It was Hillman to say that Mr. Kinnaird was asking for Mr. Mappin. Kinnaird was Gavin's attorney, a young man. Lee went out to meet him. The two gripped hands.

"Is there anything I can do?" asked Kinnaird.

"Answer a question," said Lee. "You have his will?"

"Yes."

"Is it proper for you to tell me the provisions?"

"Surely. You and I are named as executors. It's a brief will. He leaves everything to his daughter except for two bequests. Fifty thousand dollars to the Author's League Fund, and five thousand to his servant, Robert Hillman."

"So," said Lee.

"You don't suspect that . . ."

"I suspect nothing," said Lee, "but I must look into everything."

The two men discussed the various measures that must be taken in respect to Gavin's death. When the lawyer had gone Lee addressed Hillman in his mild way.

"Hillman, tell me about Mr. Dordress' movements yesterday."

"He worked, sir, until it was time to dress for dinner. Come to think of it, he did go out for a little while in the afternoon."

"Did he say where he was going when he went out?"

"To the bank, sir."

"Any place else?"

"He didn't say, sir."

"Any visitors yesterday?"

"There are always callers, sir, but I had strict orders to say he was out. He saw only one man. Mr. Alan Talbert."

"Who's he?"

"A young fellow, a playwright, I believe. He always addressed Mr. Dordress as 'the Master.'"

"How long did he stay?"

"A few minutes only. The others who called were . . ."

"Never mind if they didn't see him. . . . Now as to last night; as I understand it, Mr. and Mrs. Townley left together; shortly afterwards Miss Garrett left; then Miss Cynthia."

"That's right, sir."

"What did you do then?"

"The hired servants had already gone, sir. I just looked around to see that everything was all right, and I went home, too. Ten to eleven it was when I left."

"How long was that after Miss Cynthia had gone?"

"Twenty minutes to half an hour, sir."

"Did you see Mr. Dordress before you left?"

"Yes, sir. Went into the studio to ask if there was anything he wanted."

"What was he doing?"

"Sitting in his big chair, sir, reading."

"Did he appear to be composed?"

"Oh yes, sir. Spoke to me quiet and friendly. Said there was nothing he wanted."

"Did you notice what he was reading?"

"No, sir. A little book with a green cover."

"He must have put it back on the shelf. It's not anywhere around now."

"Yes, sir."

"So you were the last person to see him alive," said Lee quietly.

The gaunt manservant's face broke up. He was squeezing his hands together to control their trembling. "Don't say that, sir!" he stammered. "Oh, don't say that!"

"Why not?" said Lee, affecting to be surprised.

"That's what they always say of a person when he is suspected of . . . of . . . Mr. Dordress was a good master. I have worked for him nine years. . . . How could I . . . ?"

"You are not suspected of anything," said Lee mildly. "Have you any reason to believe that Mr. Dordress did not kill himself?"

"No . . . yes . . . How should I know?" stammered Hillman. "There was bad talk here last night. You know about it."

"I know about it," said Lee dryly. "But everything points to suicide. I suspect nobody. I am investigating merely to clear up any possible doubt. Keep your mouth shut, Hillman. We must be careful not to start anything that might sully Mr. Dordress' name."

"Oh yes, sir! Did you know, sir, that Miss Garrett was overheard to threaten Mr. Dordress' life?"

"Who overheard her?" asked Lee.

"One of the waiters from Millerand's, sir. It was when she first came. Miss Garrett was the first to arrive."

"I hope the man will keep his mouth shut," said Lee.

"He said he would, sir."

Lee studied the butler. "Look at me, Hillman."

The servant tried hard to keep his eyes fixed on Lee's, but they would not obey him.

"What are you afraid of?" asked Lee.

Hillman began to tremble. "I . . . I'm not afraid, sir. Only distressed. My master . . . to go like this . . ."

Lee cut him short. "Did you know you were down in his will for five thousand dollars?"

Hillman made his face look glad and surprised, but it was not convincing. "Oh, Mr. Mappin! No, sir, I didn't know! Five thousand dollars! I can scarcely believe it!"

"It's true," said Lee, watching him.

"When will I get the money, Mr. Mappin?"

"I can't tell you exactly. In a week or two, I suppose. Have you a special need of it?"

"Yes, sir. I'm buying a little restaurant, sir."

"If Mr. Dordress had not died where would you have got the money?"

"I suppose I would have gone to the loan sharks, sir."

Taking a new line, Lee asked: "What about the boy who was on the elevator last night?"

Hillman was relieved. "Joe Dietz, sir."

"Is he a friend of yours?"

"No, sir. Not to say a friend. I never took to the boy."

"Why?"

"He's too nosey. Always making up some excuse to get into the apartment. He pesters the guests for autographs and sells them."

"Get him here if you can without arousing his suspicions. I don't want to start anybody thinking there is a mystery about Mr. Dordress' death."

"Yes, sir."

Joe Dietz was hanging around in the lobby below and Hillman was able to produce him in a few minutes. An undersized young fellow with a mean expression; sharp eyes darting in every direction. "Where is he?" he asked.

Lee ignored the question. Hillman had his ears stretched, and Lee sent him into the studio to tidy it up. To Joe he said: "Miss Dordress was the last of the guests to leave last night, and after that Hillman went home?"

"That's right, sir. Do you suspect that the boss was murdered?" he asked, licking his lips.

"No," said Lee. "Mr. Dordress killed himself. I am merely trying to establish a motive. Keep your mouth shut and I'll see that you are taken care of."

"Yes, sir. You can depend upon me, sir," said Joe fawningly.

"After Hillman had gone home did you take anybody else up to Mr. Dordress' apartment?"

"No, sir."

"What were you doing at the time?"

"I took a sleep, sir."

"Where?"

"On the bench in the elevator. I left the door open."

"Where are the stairs in this building?"

"They run up in a fireproof shaft alongside the elevator."

"Is there a door to the stairs in the foyer?"

"Yes, sir. Right beside the elevator."

"While you were sleeping couldn't somebody have come up the stairs?"

"No, sir. The door's locked. It's a spring lock. If there was a fire and the tenants run down the stairs they could open the door from the inside. But on the outside you have to have a key."

"How did Hillman look when he came to work this morning? Distressed? Excited?"

"No, sir. He looked the same as usual."

"Joe," said Lee very casually, "did you come up here to Mr. Dordress' flat last night after Hillman had gone?"

Joe became very excited. "No, sir! No, sir! What for would I come up here so late? I swear I never saw Mr. Dordress last night. May God strike me dead if I ain't telling the truth!"

"Leave God out of it," said Lee dryly. He felt that the boy was lying somewhere.

"Mr. Mappin, can I see him?" asked Joe with unpleasant eagerness.

"No," said Lee.

After the boy had gone Lee called up Stan Oberry. Stan operated a small, high-class detective agency, and Lee was accustomed to calling on him for assistance. "Stan," he said, "there are two men that I want tailed. The first is Joe Dietz, an elevator boy at — Madison Avenue. He's hanging around the lobby of the house off duty, if you can send a man over. Joe is the rat-faced one. The other man is George Hillman, Mr. Dordress' servant. He'll be busy in the house all day. While waiting for him, your man might go up to 729 Calhoun Street, the Bronx, where he lives, and pick up all he can about Hillman's family, his recent movements, and his habits generally."

"Okay, Lee."

No sooner did Lee hang up, than Siebert Ackroyd arrived.

He was terribly upset. He asked to see Cynthia. When Lee brought Cynthia to him, he apologized for having flown off the handle the night before. "I had nothing against Gavin, really," he said. "Nobody knows better than me what a fine man he was!"

CHAPTER NINE

AFTER CYNTHIA had been given an opportunity to be with her father, Gavin's body was removed to a funeral establishment. Lee received the reporters again, and answered their questions as far as he thought proper. Lee was an old hand in dealing with the press, and notwithstanding the reporters' cleverness, they were unable to extract any admission from him that there was something unexplained in the death of Gavin Dordress. By this time the news was all over town, and a long procession of callers began; Gavin's admirers, actors who had appeared in his plays, playwrights he had encouraged. None of the other guests at dinner the night before called or phoned, and Lee set out in search of them.

First to the Townley Theater where Mack maintained a luxurious suite of offices. The outer room, where a line of playwrights and actors were usually waiting, was empty now. Lee was told that Mr. Townley had telephoned he would not come to the office. Lee could not go behind that, though the frightened faces of elevator boy, receptionist, and secretary suggested that Mack was in fact in the building, Probably in one of the unbridled rages for which he was known. Lee left a note for him, and proceeded to the Townley apartment on Park Avenue. Here a wooden-faced manservant told him that Mr. Townley had gone to his office.

"There's a lack of team-work," said Lee dryly. "Is Mrs. Townley in?"

"No, sir."

"Can you tell me where she may be found?"

"I don't know, sir."

"When will she return?"

"She didn't say, sir."

While Lee was talking to the man a trunk was carried across the foyer and out through a service door. "Has Mrs. Townley left the city?" he asked at a venture.

"Well, yes, sir," admitted the servant.

"Why didn't you say so at once? Where has she gone?"

"I have not been informed, sir."

Lee could get no more out of him. Nor were the hall men any more communicative. From a booth in a drug store he called Stan Oberry again.

"Stan, I have been informed that Bea Ellerman, that is, Mrs. Mack Townley, has left town. Find out for me where she's gone. In the case of so prominent a person it ought not to be difficult. If you have a discreet man on call, let him try to find out what led to this sudden departure. A woman might get it better."

"Okay, Lee."

Then to the Hotel Conradi-Windermere where Gail Garrett leased an apartment. Lee did not send up his name, but proceeded directly to Gail's quarters in the tower. The door was opened by Gail's own maid, Catherine, who was known to Lee. The elderly woman was pale and shaken. Lee made believe not to notice anything out of the way.

"Good morning, Catherine. I'd like to see Miss Garrett for a moment."

"She's not in," muttered Catherine.

Lee could hear Gail's voice behind the closed door of the living-room. He pushed past Catherine. After all, he had known Gail Garrett for fifteen years.

"It won't do you no good!" complained Catherine. "She won't see you. She won't see nobody!"

"She is seeing somebody now," said Lee.

"It's Mr. Bittner from the theater."

Lee seated himself in the foyer. "I will wait until she is free."

Catherine, wringing her hands together, went away through a service door.

Lee heard the rumble of a man's voice behind the living-room door. The words were indistinguishable. Then Gail's voice, shrill and strident:

"I don't care! I won't appear. I won't! All right, put a notice in the paper; return the money. Don't you think I have any feelings?" Another rumble.

"Get out! You're driving me mad! Get out! Get out, you fool! Close the show. I will never act again! Never! Never! I'm through!"

Little Solon Bittner, Gail Garrett's producer, came out of the living-room very red in the face. The door slammed behind him. The two men nodded to each other; Bittner said to Lee with a desperate air: "She refuses to go on tonight. She wants me to close the show. You are her friend. Try to get her to listen to reason."

"Give her a little time, Bittner," said Lee. "She's had a terrible shock."

"But if Miss Garrett is unable to go on because Gavin Dordress shoots himself, it will make a scandal. It will injure her."

Lee shrugged.

The little man went on out, waving his hands.

Lee knocked on the living-room door. "Gail, it's me, Lee Mappin."

"Go away!" answered a strangled voice.

"Sorry, I have to talk to you. It's imperative."

"Go away!"

Lee opened the door and walked in. The great, beautiful room, decorated in the style of Louis Seize by a master, was all in disorder. One of the gilt chairs was overthrown; clothes, pillows, torn papers were scattered about. Gail, wearing an elaborate negligee, sat crouched in a chair bent almost double, as if in physical pain. In her hands she had a handkerchief that she was slowly tearing into shreds. Her face was ravaged—by grief, rage, fear; it was impossible to tell which; perhaps all three. She looked terrible and she didn't care.

"Get out!" she said sullenly, with scarcely a glance at Lee. "I told you not to come in. Have I no privacy in my own home? Can't I ever be left alone?"

"I'm sorry," said Lee, "but you must listen to me for a few moments." He sat down.

She sprang up in a rage. "Must? Must? I'm not accustomed to that sort of talk and I'm not going to take it from you! Leave my rooms or I'll telephone to the office and have you put out!"

Lee faced her out. "You're only making a show of yourself," he said calmly. "If you will stop to think, you must realize that I have always been your friend, that I was Gavin's friend. Now I have work to do. There is reason to believe that Gavin did not kill himself."

He noted that she was not surprised. She started to pace. "What difference does it make?" she mourned. "He is gone and nothing can bring him back to me."

"Last night you were overheard to threaten his life," said Lee.

That arrested her attention. She stopped, staring at him wildly, pressing her face between her hands. "Overheard? By whom?"

"One of the waiters hired for the evening."

Gail sneered. "It's a lie! He can't prove it!"

"He can testify to it."

"Nobody would believe a waiter!"

"Unfortunately, there were other unpleasant incidents. The scene when you left."

"Who would dare to accuse me?" she demanded.

"My dear," said Lee dryly, "nobody is safe from an accusation."

"What did you come here for?" she asked sharply.

"To get you to tell me the truth as far as you knew it. . . . What did you do when you left Gavin's last night?"

"I came home."

"Right away?"

"Just as quick as a taxi could bring me."

"Did you enter the hotel through the lobby?"

"I never use the lobby. I came in the private entrance for the tower apartments."

"There are two elevators," said Lee. "Which one did you use? Right or left as you face them?"

Gail's lip curled. "I suppose you are going to verify my statements by questioning the elevator boys."

"Surely."

"All right. I came up in the left-hand elevator. And it was operated by the one they call Vincent, one of the older employees. I hope you're satisfied."

"Thank you," said Lee. "Did you go out again later?"

Gail bit her lip, hesitated, blurted out:

"I *did* go out again."

"Where did you go?"

"I won't tell you."

"That looks bad, Gail."

"I don't care how it looks. I was on my own private business."

"For your own sake I ask you to tell me," Lee said. "After all these years you must know that you can trust me."

"You'll get no more out of me," she said with tight lips.

Lee got up. "Then I'll have to find out through other sources."

"I wish you luck."

"I met Bittner outside," said Lee. "The poor fellow was in despair. Of course he stands to lose a fortune if you insist on his closing the show."

"Closing the show?" said Gail sharply. "Whoever suggested such a thing?"

"You did."

"Oh, for God's sake!" she cried melodramatically, "why must you all take me so literally! I'm not going to close the show. I'm a good trouper. I shall go on as usual tonight, though my heart is breaking!"

"Then you'd better telephone him," Lee suggested dryly.

Through one of the managers of the hotel who was an acquaintance, Lee got in touch with Vincent, the elevator boy. Vincent told him that he had taken up Miss Garrett about ten thirty the previous night, and almost immediately afterwards had carried her down again. She had taken a taxi at the private door. It was a driver who regularly served the hotel, and Vincent was able to give Lee his name. Later in the afternoon the taxi-driver came to Lee's office and told the following story:

"Miss Gail Garrett hired me at the private door of the Conradi-Windermere about twenty to eleven. I recognized her from her pictures. She looked bad. I thought she had been drinking. She told

me to take her to — Bayard Street on the East Side. That's a bad
neighborhood. Near Chinatown. The Nonpareil Social Club occu-
pies two floors at that number. She sent me in to ask for a guy
named 'Cagey.' He was there, playing pool, and I brought him out
to her . . ."

"What sort of fellow?" interrupted Lee.

"He was well named," said the taxi-driver. "Gangster, if I know
anything. A slick, smooth young guy with a wall eye. Swell dresser.
Eyetalian descent. A two-gun man, by the look of him.

"He leans in the back of the cab and talks to her. I can't hear
much, but I makes out he's bawling her out for coming to him and
leaving a wide-open trail. Seemed funny a young East Side guy
would have the face to talk to Gail Garrett like that. I figures he
must have something on her. Well, she gets out and pays me, and I
drive away."

"Damn!" muttered Lee. "Didn't you realize that you were on
the track of something? Didn't you watch them?"

The driver compressed his lips. "Sure I thought it was funny,
but it wasn't none of my business. Us hackies can't afford to get
nosey, Mister."

Lee gave him a tip and promised that there would be more in it
for him later if he kept his mouth shut.

Lee phoned to Stan Oberry for a report on the youth known as
"Cagey" who was a member of the Nonpareil Social Club in Bayard
Street. Within a couple of hours he was in possession of the fol-
lowing:

> "Francesco Chigi (American pronunciation 'Cagey')
> known also as Frank Chigi, Cecco Chigi, and Cagey
> Frank. Twenty-three years old; born at — Mulberry
> Street, where his parents still live, but they have not
> seen him since he came out of prison. A dangerous
> man. Is said to derive a good income from victimiz-
> ing wealthy women. Several such are known to have
> fallen for his good looks."

CHAPTER TEN

WHEN LEE RETURNED to the Dordress apartment the nervous Hillman said that Mr. Mack Townley had not called on the phone. Mr. Emmett Gundy was waiting in the sunroom. Lee went in to Emmett. No matter how poor Emmett was, he contrived to be well dressed. He would have gone without food sooner than show himself otherwise. He was wearing the blue fur overcoat which Lee thought silly. Lee had known him for twenty-five years, but had not seen much of him lately. Out-of-doors with his hat on, Emmett could still pass for a handsome young man. But of late his face had taken on the sour look of one who feels that he is not appreciated. He said the things that Lee had already listened to twenty times that day.

"What a terrible thing, Lee! Little did I think last night that I would never see Gavin again! I can scarcely realize that he's gone. Every moment I expect to see him come walking out of the studio. I didn't hear of it until I went out at noon. Why didn't you send for me? Is there anything I can do?"

Emmett had always been like that—self-centered. He couldn't get excited about anything except what concerned himself. Lee sat down, suddenly conscious of an immense weariness. He had had no time to indulge his own grief. "There is nothing to do," he said. "It has all been taken care of. . . . But I'd like to ask you a question or two."

"Sure," said Emmett, "anything at all."

"You were one of Gavin's closest friends; first I must tell you there is a suspicion that he may not have killed himself."

"I'm not surprised," said Emmett. "There were ugly passions brewing here last night. . . . What evidence have you?"

"Practically none. It is chiefly Cynthia. She refuses to believe that her father killed himself."

"That's natural enough," said Emmett. "Maybe when she gets over the shock she'll forget her suspicions."

"Maybe."

"What did you want of me?"

"You and Louella Kip were the first ones to leave here after dinner last night. Where did you go?"

Emmett smiled thinly. "You don't think that I . . . ?"

"No! No!" said Lee wearily.

"Gavin has been practically keeping me for the last three months. It's not likely that . . ."

"Of course not. But answer the question."

"I told Gavin we were going on to another party," said Emmett. "That was just an excuse to get away. As a matter of fact, Louella and I went directly to my place. I had been discussing with her some changes I was going to make in my novel, and we got out the script and went to work on it. We got so interested in it we worked for three or four hours. It was two o'clock before she went home."

"Where is your place?" asked Lee.

"It's a dump on East Thirty-fourth Street," said Emmett. "Number —. Just one room. I've been so broke lately I couldn't afford anything better."

"Walk-up?"

"Sure."

"Did anybody see you come in, or see Louella leave?"

"I doubt it."

"Where does Louella live?"

"In a boarding-house on Irving Place. Mrs. Cayley's."

"Thanks," said Lee.

He got up to indicate that he was finished, but Emmett lingered. "Have you any theory as to what happened?" he asked.

"None whatever," said Lee. "I'm just working to satisfy Cynthia."

Still Emmett made no move to go. Finally he said: "I'm in a hell of a hole, Lee. These circulating libraries are ruining us novelists. More people are reading my novels than ever before, but my royalties are only a third of what they were. Gavin had promised to lend me a hundred to tide me over until I could collect my next advance. I was to see him at five today. I don't know what I'll do now."

Lee thought: Always the same Emmett. He makes a touch with the air of one conferring a favor. He drew out his checkbook. "Let me take his place," he said.

"That certainly is good of you, Lee. I'll pay it back just as soon as I place my novel."

When he had gone, Lee looked up Mrs. Cayley's number in the phone-book. In due course he heard Louella's gentle voice on the wire, and his face softened; he liked Louella; everybody liked her. Her voice now was shaken with distress.

"Oh, Mr. Mappin, I can't tell you how dreadfully I feel about Mr. Dordress! To have this happen so soon after we had seen him! I didn't know him very well, but he was always so kind, so warmhearted, so generous, I felt as if he was one of my dearest friends

There was no doubt of the genuineness of Louella's feelings. Lee said, as if it were a matter of small concern: "There are various points in connection with last night that I have to check up. You understand it's purely a formality. Where did you and Emmett when you left Gavin's?"

"We went direct to Emmett's place," she said, quickly. "He wanted to read me part of his new novel and ask my advice about changing it. We got so interested in it we worked over it for three hours or more. It was nearly two when I got home."

"Do you room alone?" asked Lee.

"Yes," she said in a surprised voice. "Why do you ask that?"

"Did anybody in the boarding-house see you come in?"

"Oh no! At that hour it's like a house of the dead." An agitated note came into her voice. "Why do you ask me these questions, Mr. Mappin? Is there anything wrong? Is there . . ."

"No, indeed!" said Lee soothingly. "It's just a formality."

She did not sound altogether reassured. However, he bade her good- by and hung up.

Lee, looking for Mack Townley, called up his office, his home, the Racquet Club, where he was accustomed to play hand-ball in the afternoon; the Federal League Club. He was said not to be at any of these places, nor would anyone tell Lee where he might be found. There could be no doubt that Mack was deliberately keeping out of the way.

Before he was married, Mack had hung out for years at the Federal League Club, and Lee had a hunch that he would fly back there like a homing pigeon. He decided to take a chance on it. Putting on hat and coat again, he had himself driven to the magnificent quarters of the Federal League on Park Avenue.

To the boy at the desk he said offhandedly: "Mr. Townley phoned me to come here for a conference. I'll go right up to his room."

Lee had the kind of front that impresses club servants, and the boy never thought of questioning his statement. As he started up in the elevator, Lee said suddenly:

"There! I've forgotten the number they gave me at the desk!"

"Whose room, sir?" asked the elevator man.

"Mr. Townley's."

"Number seventeen, sir."

Lee knocked on the door of seventeen and Mack's sullen voice answered, "Who is it?"

Lee smiled to himself at the success of his ruse. "Lee Mappin," he said, and went in without waiting to be bidden.

Mack Townley's heavy face was a study when he saw Lee. He was trying to make out that he was glad to see him, but he could not control the flush of anger. He sat relaxed and glooming in an easy-chair by the window. There was a whisky-bottle on a stand within reach of his hand.

"Hello!" he growled. "I've been trying to get hold of you all day."

Lee's bland expression suggested: Not too hard, I think! He said: "I've been trying to get hold of you, too."

Lee was shocked by the change that only eighteen hours had worked in Mack. His face was ravaged as if by disease. The glass when he lifted it to his lips trembled violently in his hand.

"Have a drink," he growled. "You'll find another glass in the bathroom."

"No, thanks," said Lee. "You know me. I can't drink hard liquor before dinner."

"God, Lee, this is a frightful blow to me! I can't face it!"

This sounded like something Lee had heard a short time before. These mourners for Gavin's death thought first of themselves, it seemed.

"I got in a rage with Gavin last night," Mack went on. "I cursed him when I left him. And then to hear that he was dead—God! it was as if I had killed him by wishing him dead!" Mack, clenching his fist until the knuckles whitened, pounded his knee. "God, Lee, I've been in hell all day! I've been in hell!"

"Mack," said Lee, "there is a suspicion that Gavin did not kill himself."

Mack's face flushed in a terrible manner that made it look blackish. "Is there any evidence that he was put out of the way," he demanded harshly, "or do you suspect me just because I cursed him last night?"

Lee faced him out. "Not much evidence," he said. "Did you read the letter he left?"

"Yes. It was in the paper."

"It does not ring true," said Lee. "It is too general in its terms."

"Who's to say it doesn't ring true? Gavin was a queer fellow at heart."

"Mack," said Lee quietly, "what did you do when you left Gavin's apartment last night?"

Mack's face turned black again. He half hoisted himself out of his chair, then dropped back into it heavily. "I suppose you've got the right to suspect me," he growled . . . "after the way I talked. God knows I had the will to kill Gavin last night . . . but I didn't do it."

"Where did you go?" persisted Lee.

"Bea and I drove home to our apartment," Mack answered with a defiant glare. "We went directly to bed. I read for a while and then I slept. And that's that."

"Where's Bea?" asked Lee.

Mack scowled at him. "Have you been looking for her?"

"Naturally,"

Mack hesitated before he answered, drawing his hand down over his face. "When Bea heard this morning what had happened she was in a state of collapse. I have put her in a sanatorium to save her from prying eyes."

"Where?" asked Lee.

"I won't tell you that. Not even you. I promised her."

"You realize, of course, that Bea is the only one who can support the alibi you have offered."

"All right," growled Mack, "if you want to bring a charge against me, Bea will appear."

"I don't want to bring a charge against you," said Lee. "I want you to give me the facts that will clear you once and for all."

"I'll satisfy you tomorrow," muttered Mack. "Just give me time to get my grip."

Lee glanced at the whisky-bottle, but said nothing.

"I'm not the only one that had it in for Gavin," growled Mack.

"I'm following up every line," said Lee.

"Here's something you don't know," said Mack. "A week ago Gail Garrett came to me to borrow a thousand dollars. I said: 'Good God, Gail! Bittner is paying you fifteen hundred a week, and twenty-five per cent of the net. The show is making money. Where has it all gone?' She said: 'It's my debts, Mack; they're keeping me poor.'"

"How do you figure that this connects Gail with what happened last night?" asked Lee.

Mack said meaningly: "In this town there are guns for hire, Lee. They come high. Suppose Gail was getting the money together to hire a gun?"

"Did you let her have the thousand?"

"No. I have other uses for my money."

"I'll look into it," said Lee. "What day did she come to you?"

"Last Monday," said Mack, "the seventh."

Upon leaving Mack, Lee went to his office on Madison Avenue near by, to see if anything had come in. He found three reports waiting for him. The first:

> "I picked up Joe Dietz at — Madison Avenue and kept him under observation until he started away at 2 P.M. He took the subway to the Bushwick section of Brooklyn, where he lives. He entered a large pool-room at — Marcy Avenue and played pool. Joe was quite the hero of the hour. He claimed to be a personal friend of Mr. Dordress', but it sounded phony to me. He was acting mysterious, sort of letting on that it was no suicide if the truth was known, and he, Joe, knew enough to bust the case wide open if he wanted to speak. My opinion, is he was just running his lip, as they say. They only thing funny about him is that he certainly has more money to spend than the 18 or 20 a week he pulls down as an elevator man."
>
> "J. B."

The second report:

> "According to instructions I proceeded to 729 Calhoun Street, the Bronx. It is a five-story walk-up apartment house for thirty families. Pretty cheap rents. There is no family by the name of Hillman living there now. The janitor told me they moved away about six weeks ago. He didn't know their present address. I got some of their old neighbors in talk. Hillman family consisted of father, mother, and a boy and girl of high school age. The father a quiet man, worked long hours and was rarely seen. His wife gave out that he was in the theatrical business.

Mrs. Hillman was not popular with the neighbors, being considered too ritzy. Was always boasting about her rich friends. At the time they moved she told her neighbors that they were in the money now and would be living in a much better style hereafter. She did not tell anybody where they were going. On inquiring at the post-office I found they had left no forwarding address. When Hillman leaves his work tonight I will tail him to his new home.

"R. S."

The third report:

"I ran down the driver of the taxi who carried Mr. and Mrs. Mack Townley from — Madison Avenue to the Andorra Apartments last night shortly before ten thirty. His name is Dave Levine, of — Scammell Street. Levine told me that the couple quarreled so loudly on the way home that he could hear part of what they said. T. was jealous; accused his wife of being too friendly with Gavin Dordress. She threatened to leave him. At the Andorra Mrs. Townley went straight in, but Townley, when he had paid the driver, walked away down Park in a blind rage. Tappan, night hall man at the Andorra, told me Townley returned at 3 A.M. As Tappan put it, he looked as if he'd been through the mill. Townley, still in a rage, left the house again about eight-forty. Two hours later Mrs. Townley called a cab and had herself driven to Grand Central Station. She bought a ticket to Reno, Nevada, and engaged space right through. Her trunks were sent after her. I got next to Cabbett, the butler, at the Townleys', but he wouldn't talk. I'll try to get a line on the other servants.

"A."

Lee sat for a while, smoking and studying. Finally, he put the reports in his pocket and went on to the Dordress apartment. His first thought there was to consult the stubs in Gavin's current checkbook. He discovered that on November 7th Gavin had issued a check to "G. G." for a thousand dollars. Lee's face turned pretty grim.

CHAPTER ELEVEN

LEE MAPPIN and Cynthia met in the sunroom. Under Cynthia's direction Hillman was watering the rare ferns and tropical plants that had been Gavin's pride. Cynthia was moving about, pinching off a dead leaf here and there, and tying up the plants that were too heavy for their stems. At five o'clock she had insisted on letting Fanny go home.

"Dad used to do this every afternoon," she said with a painful smile. When Hillman had finished his job and departed, she wanted to know what had happened. Lee hesitated.

"Tell me," she said.

He did so.

Cynthia's pale face, refined by grief, turned hard. "It was Gail Garrett," she murmured. "That's clear!"

"Keep an open mind!" Lee warned her, "until we turn up the final positive proof."

Later Lee said: "If you have no objections, I would like to send to my place for a bag and sleep here for the next few nights."

"Objections? Of course not! But why, Lee?"

"I don't feel that I have got all the evidence that these rooms may contain, and I don't like to leave the place unguarded."

"I'll stay here with you if you want me," said Cynthia.

"Very good idea," said Lee. "In your own place the reporters would continually be ringing your phone and your door-bell. I didn't suggest it because I thought it might be painful for you."

Lee and Cynthia dined quietly together that evening. Each had a burden of grief to bear, and each was comforted by the other's presence. Neither felt obliged to talk. When the meal came to an end Lee told Hillman he could go home as soon as he had cleaned up. Lee and Cynthia started going over Gavin's papers in the studio.

"Hadn't I better do this first alone?" asked Lee, "We may stumble on painful things."

Cynthia shook her head. "Everything that concerns Dad is dear to me," she said. "I don't care what we may find."

Hillman left about eight-thirty. Half an hour later Lee was called to the phone. It was Stan Oberry.

"I'm sorry I have to report a slip-up," he said. "When Hillman came out of the Madison Avenue house he dived into a taxicab bound westward. He had evidently been standing inside the door, watching the traffic lights and timed his exit so that he got a cab and across Madison without delay. Schelling, my operative, says that Hillman couldn't have seen him. Hillman was expecting to be tailed, and took his measures accordingly. Schelling got another cab and followed, but lost some precious time. Hillman dismissed his cab at Times Square and ran down one of the subway entrances. Schelling followed, but lost him in the station. That place, as you know, is like a rabbit warren. Schelling says he is sure that Hillman merely ran down one flight of steps and up another. Schelling got a place where he could watch both platforms, and he did not see Hillman take a train."

"That's all right," said Lee. "Operatives are only human. Let Schelling try to tail Hillman again tomorrow. Or, if he has any reason to believe that Hillman spotted him, put another man on Hillman's tail."

"Okay," said Stan.

In half an hour he called Lee again. "Better luck this time," he said. "Frank Chigi, or Cagey, turned up in Hester Street awhile ago and has taken his girl out to dinner. Cagey is lousy with money. He brought the girl a fur coat that must have set him back three hundred dollars or more. He has taken her to André's, a French restaurant in Park Row, and is buying champagne. My operative, Vosper, is watching the place. What do you want me to do? I've got a man here that I can send down to Vosper with instructions. Do you want to question this Cagey?"

"Sure," said Lee quickly. "Maybe the champagne will loosen his tongue. The opportunity is too good to be passed up. Who is the man you've got there in your office?"

"Schelling."

"All right. Let Schelling go down to the door and I'll pick him up in three minutes. He can come downtown with me and introduce me to Vosper, and we'll work out something together. You had better stay in your office until you hear from me."

"Right!"

Cynthia was distressed. "No, Lee, no!" she protested. "Let Mr. Oberry do it, or one of his men. That's their work. This man Cagey is dangerous. He is known as a killer."

"He won't hurt me," said Lee smiling. "I shall pose as the most harmless little gentleman that ever took a drop too much. Cagey is too important to turn over to anybody else."

Quarter of an hour later Lee and Schelling got out of a taxi at the Park Row entrance to the Brooklyn Bridge and walked on to André's restaurant at the corner of Frankfort Street. In this neighborhood there are always plenty of people about. At the top of the steps leading to the basement restaurant they ran into Vosper, Stan Oberry's other operative. Lee was introduced to Vosper, and the latter said:

"They're still inside."

"Good," said Lee. "I'm going in to try to get next to them. You two men take cover and wait for us to come out. If I am with the couple, follow us wherever we may go. If they won't let me go with them, you follow them, and communicate with me when you can through Stan's office."

"Okay, Mr. Mappin."

Lee, pulling a lock of hair over his forehead, and setting his derby and his necktie slightly askew, went down the steps and entered the little restaurant with a rolling gait and an expression of great dignity. Occasionally he hiccupped behind his hand. He represented a type that is dear to all waiters, and the two waiters in the place hastened forward to assist him tenderly to a seat. Lee paused, swaying on his feet, and looked around him. It was well past the usual dinner hour and there were only three couples left in the place. He had no difficulty in picking out the one he wanted. Disregarding the suggestions of the waiters, he rolled up to the next table and sat down. A menu card was thrust under his nose.

"Don't wanna eat. Wanna drink," said Lee, hiccupping. "Gimme Black and White highball."

"Yes, sir."

It was a comely couple at the next table. Lee's seeming drunken glance was all over the place, but he missed no detail. The young man's trim, muscular figure was set off by a well-cut brown suit. He wore a snowy shirt that emphasized his smooth, swarthy skin and an orange tie from an expensive shop. His blue-black hair glistened like steel under the lights. He affected an absolutely dead pan. The girl, who was about his own age, and like him of Italian extraction, was pretty in a cheap fashion, and very smartly turned out. Her hat had an upstanding brim that enframed her pert face like a halo. Over the back of her chair was flung a costly leopard coat. Cagey addressed her as Clo-Clo. She was crazy about her dangerous little boy friend, and could not hide it. He accepted it as his due.

Lee noticed that Cagey was not drinking. Occasionally he tasted his wine, no more. On the other hand, Clo-Clo loved it as women love champagne. Cagey filled her glass from time to time, and already her face was flushed and her tongue unloosed. She leaned across the table and spoke to Cagey. Lee could read her lips.

"Take a look at the comical little rummy who just come in."

Cagey glanced at Lee indifferently. His eyes had the yellow flicker of a cat animal after feeding. Lee's drink had just been put before him. He raised it with drunken solemnity and toasted Cagey. The young man merely stared. But the girl was interested.

"Hey, Daddy, drink with me!" she said.

Lee's line was the old-fashioned drunk. "'S a privilege," he said, bowing to Cagey, "if the young gen'leman will permit."

Cagey's glance was contemptuous. "Sure," he said.

Lee raised his glass. "To your pretty eyes!"

Clo-Clo giggled. "Ain't he the gentleman!"

"Gen'leman enough to reco'nize a lady when I see one!" said Lee.

Clo-Clo leaned across the table to whisper to Cagey. Lee guessed that she was saying the old guy looked like he might be carrying a roll. Cagey shrugged. Clo-Clo said:

"Come on over, Daddy!"

Thus Lee found himself sitting between them and sharing the wine. He accepted a second glass. He and Clo-Clo made the confused noises that pass for conversation on such occasions, while Cagey listened with a sneer.

Cagey was sober. Sober and watchful. Lee said: "Wassa matter, young man? You're not drinking wine. Want you join me drinking health this beauriful girl!" He toasted Clo-Clo.

Cagey tasted his wine and put the glass down.

"Bottoms up! Bottoms up!" cried Lee. "She's worth it, isn't she? Don't tell me young fellow like you can't 'preciate such beauriful girl!"

Cagey was annoyed. His eyes flickered dangerously.

"Ah, leave him be," said Clo-Clo to Lee. "You and me can finish the bottle. Frank's got a job of work tonight and he don't want to . . ."

The sleepy yellow eyes suddenly blazed, and by the girl's suppressed cry it was evident that Cagey had stamped on her foot under the table. Lee hiccupped.

"Job of work," he muttered. "Good boy! I honor the workers. What's your line, young man?"

"I'm a printer on the *Daily American*," said Cagey. "I go on at eleven o'clock. That's what Clo-Clo meant by a job of work."

Lee appeared to be satisfied. "Time for another bottle," he said.

Cagey glanced at his watch: "I got to leave you," he said, "you and Clo-Clo can drink it."

Lee rubbed his lip. "She is beauriful girl!" he murmured.

Clo-Clo slipped her arm through his. "Say, this dump is as gay as a funeral parlor. You come with me, Daddy, and I'll show you something."

When their waiter brought the check, Cagey coolly signified that Lee would pay it. The three of them then left the place together. On the way out Cagey, with a hard look at Clo-Clo, whispered something to her out of the corner of his mouth. Lee couldn't hear it, but he got her reply:

"I'll take care of him."

On the street Cagey bade them a casual good-by and struck off across Park Row in the direction of a subway entrance. This was not the way to reach the *American* building, of course. Lee had to let him go. However, he saw Stan's men, Vosper and Schelling, converging on the subway entrance from different directions.

CHAPTER TWELVE

LEE AND CLO-CLO WAITED at the curb for a taxi. Lee suspected that the girl, like himself, was not so tight as she was making out to be.

As she leaned against him he was aware of her light fingers touching his different pockets to find out where he kept his roll. As a matter of fact, his wallet was in his breast pocket, and as his jacket was buttoned across, it was not too easy to get at.

A cab came and Clo-Clo gave a number in Bayard Street.

They finally drew up before the side door of a Chinese resort that fronted on Mott Street. Lee paid off the taxi.

"Chinatown?" he muttered as he stood swaying on the sidewalk. "Don't like Chinatown. It's nasty. Le's go decent place."

Clo-Clo slipped her arm through his. "Come on, Daddy," she said cajolingly. "This is a real nice place. Only white people come here. Would I bring you here if it wasn't nice?"

Lee stood his ground. Clo-Clo suddenly dropped Lee's arm and, cursing him, went through the door of a saloon and slammed it after her.

The instant she disappeared, Lee recovered his sobriety. Without waiting, lest Clo-Clo return, he hastened right through to the Bowery and from a booth in a drug store called up Stan Oberry's office. He gave Stan a brief account of what had happened. Stan, it appeared, had not yet heard from Schelling and Vosper. Lee gave Stan the number of his pay station, and stood by, waiting for him to call again.

In five minutes or so the call came through. Stan said:

"Cagey took a subway express to the One Hundred Seventy-seventh Street station in the Bronx. Schelling says the train was full and Cagey didn't get on to the fact that he was being tailed. From the subway station he proceeded on foot to Ingoldsby Avenue. This street faces Bronx Park. Number thirty-three Ingoldsby is Cagey's mark. He walked around it, taking a slant from every side, then crossed over to the Park. He is lying on a bank below the street level, watching the house. There are lights in the upstairs windows. He is up to mischief of some sort. Schelling left Vosper watching Cagey and went to telephone. Schelling will stand by the telephone for five minutes for instructions. If you want to come up there he says meet him at the corner of Ingoldsby and One Hundred Seventy-ninth Street. That corner is outside Cagey's line of vision."

Lee said to Stan: "Phone Schelling that if he and Vosper are satisfied that a serious crime is contemplated, it's up to them to prevent it. That comes first. Meanwhile, I'll get up there as quick as I can. Subway express is the quickest. I'll be at the meeting-place in twenty-five minutes. After you've talked to Schelling, find out from the telephone company who lives at thirty-three Ingoldsby Avenue. Use my name."

Lee met Schelling at the corner of two empty streets. It was one of the older and pleasanter neighborhoods of the Bronx, removed from the crowded blocks of flats. Across the road stretched the dark expanse of Bronx Park with street lamps at intervals.

"Anything new?" asked Lee.

"No," said Schelling. "When I left, Cagey was still watching the house. Waiting for the lights to go out."

He led Lee across into the Park, which sloped down from the street level. For a few hundred feet they followed one of the footpaths which ran parallel with the street above. The other side of the street was lined with a row of semi-detached suburban houses. It was not yet midnight, and there were still a few couples sitting on the park benches or strolling along. Watching his chance, Schelling pulled Lee behind a clump of shrubbery at a moment when they were unobserved. From this clump they gained another, nearer to the street fence, and so came to the spot where Schelling had left his mate on watch.

"Vosper's gone!" he whispered.

A moment later they discovered him lying in the spot where Cagey had been.

"Cagey's just gone across the road," Vosper whispered. "He sneaked around behind thirty-three. The lights have gone out."

"This lad's line is more likely to be murder than robbery," said Lee. "Quick, we must divide here. Schelling, you go in search of a policeman. Vosper, you sneak back under the fence and cut across the street below, where he can't see you. I'll go the other way. Work back under the rear walls of the houses and we'll meet at the back door of thirty-three!"

Lee ran along under the fence for a hundred feet, then made his way across the street and between two of the houses opposite. He thought: For an amateur this is getting too close to crime. The back yards had been thrown into a community garden; there were no fences. A certain amount of light from the street struck in between each pair of houses. Lee crept back along a garden path towards thirty-three. As he approached the house, he sensed Vosper coming from the other direction.

There was a little platform at each kitchen door and on the platform of thirty-three rose a dark object which might have been a garbage can. But certain movements betrayed it. It was Cagey squatting down, apparently working at the lock of the kitchen door. As Lee drew closer the door opened. Cagey stood up and took a swift survey of the garden while Lee flattened himself against the wall. Cagey entered the house, leaving the door open.

Lee and Vosper ran silently for the steps. Lee got there first. "Watch out! Watch out!" Vosper whispered urgently, but Lee, disregarding the warning, sprang up the steps and ran into the kitchen.

"There's a robber in the house!" he called out. "Turn on lights!"

They heard a thump, as of somebody leaping out of bed upstairs, then silence in the dark house. Somewhere near, they knew

Cagey was crouching, breathing fast. The plan of the little house was apparent at a glance. Lee and Vosper were in the kitchen. As they faced the front, there was a swing door into the dining-room to the left and a door into the hall to the right. This door stood open. Looking through the hall they could see the street lights through the panes of the front door. Lee and Vosper waited, one on each side of the hall door. Vosper had a gun in his hand.

Up-stairs a switch clicked, and the lower hall was flooded with light. They saw the natty figure of Cagey crouching near the foot of the stairs. His dark face was like a waxen mask with only the eyes alive. Holding his gun poised, his eyes darted this way and that, but he could find nothing to shoot at. He backed to the front door.

"Lend me your gun," whispered Lee to Vosper.

The gun was shoved into his hand, and he slipped noiselessly through the swing door into the dining-room. There was an arched opening between the dining-room and living-room, and on the right of the living-room, another arch into the hall. By creeping around the wall, Lee got within ten feet of Cagey; near enough to see the young man's breast rising and falling with his panting breath. Cagey with his free hand was feeling behind him for the lock of the front door. Lee said:

"Drop your gun! I have you covered."

Instead of obeying, Cagey dived for the stairs, and started scrambling up on all fours. Lee could not shoot because of the intervening banisters. A gun barked from the head of the stairs. Cagey rose to his full height with his arms flung above his head. He crashed over backwards and slid to the foot, where he lay huddled, with blood running down his face and onto the gay orange tie. His gun had flown out of his hand. Lee walked out, and picking it up stood looking down at him. He was dead. Vosper joined him from the kitchen.

"A handsome lad," muttered Lee. "Too bad he couldn't have been used for a better purpose."

Hearing a sound from the top of the stairs, he looked up. He saw a gray-faced man in pajamas with a gun hanging down from his shaking hand. It was George Hillman. The two men stared at each other. Lee, who was fond of saying that nothing could surprise him, was, for once, brought up all standing. Hillman gasped out:

"Mr. Mappin . . . how did you get here?"

"What are you doing here?" said Lee.

"I live here, sir."

Lee looked around at the expensively furnished rooms with a grim expression. He indicated the body at his feet. "Do you know this man?"

"No, sir! No, sir!" protested Hillman breathlessly. "I never saw him before. He is just a robber, a common robber. He broke into my house; he had a gun in his hand; I had a right to shoot him."

"Surely," said Lee. "Come down and look at him closer."

Hillman slowly descended the stairs.

"You were expecting some such attack?"

"No, sir! No, sir! Why should anybody attack me?"

"That's what I want to know . . . why the gun?"

"I'm a timid man, sir. I always keep a gun handy."

"Why did he choose this house instead of one of the others? What have you of special value that he was after?"

"Nothing, sir, nothing! You can search the place and see for yourself."

They heard steps on the porch outside and there was a heavy pounding on the front door. It was Schelling bringing a policeman. Soon afterwards two more officers arrived in a radio car. The neighbors, in various states of undress, gathered on the porch, peeping through the windows with inquisitive and terrified eyes.

The body was removed to the police station and the whole party accompanied it. This was very awkward for Lee, who dreaded the exposure of a scandal that would involve Gavin Dordress. Lee said that he was on his way to see Hillman about a matter concerning his late master's affairs. He had seen the dead man acting suspiciously and had called on two strangers (Vosper and Schelling) for aid. Vosper and Schelling lied as to the nature of their occupations. Hillman was only too glad to support this story. He produced a license to carry a gun. Lee noted that it was dated a month before. The affair was treated as a simple burglary. The butler was allowed to go on his own recognizance. Indeed, the police lieutenant congratulated him on his presence of mind. The dead man was removed to the Morgue to await identification.

When they left the police station Lee sent Vosper and Schelling home, and took Hillman into a saloon on Fordham Avenue. Lee had reason to believe that Mrs. Hillman wore the trousers of the family, and he wanted to question the husband alone. Hillman was obviously dreading it. He swallowed a shot of whisky to give him courage.

"Hillman," began Lee, "where did you get the money to live in such style?"

"My wife and I operate a restaurant," Hillman answered nervously. "I told you that, Mr. Mappin."

"No, you didn't," said Lee. "You told me you had paid something down on a restaurant, and still required a large sum to conclude the deal."

"We took possession when I made the first payment. I just omitted to state that. I wasn't trying to deceive you, Mr. Mappin."

"An important omission," said Lee. "Where did you get the money to make the first payment?"

"It was the savings of a lifetime, Mr. Mappin. I have been putting by money since I was a boy."

"How could you keep a family on a hundred and fifty a month and put by money?"

"My wife helped me. She works, too."

In Lee's report on the Hillmans there had been no mention that Mrs. Hillman was a wage-earner. "How much did you pay down?" asked Lee.

"Only one thousand dollars, sir. We are paying off the balance out of earnings."

"Where is this restaurant?"

"On Jerome Park Avenue, Mr. Mappin. It is called Harvest's."

"Who did you buy it from?"

"Howard Harvest, sir. Hiss address is — Webster Avenue."

"Why did you never tell Mr. Dordress that you were engaging in business?"

"Why, sir, I was afraid Mr. Dordress might resent it because I was getting ready to leave him. I had been working for him nine years, you see."

"Well, why didn't you leave him?"

"I just couldn't bring myself to it, Mr. Mappin. After nine years it was like second nature to me to be waiting on Mr. Dordress."

"Never mind the nine years," said Lee. "Tell me plainly why, when you were in receipt of a good income from the restaurant, you were willing to go on slaving for twelve or fourteen hours a day for a hundred and fifty a month."

"I wasn't sure we could make a go of the restaurant," said Hillman faintly.

"Have you been stealing from Mr. Dordress?" asked Lee bluntly.

"No, sir! No, sir!" protested Hillman. "How can you say such a thing, Mr. Mappin?"

"If you have been guilty of any minor crimes you had better say so."

"Mr. Mappin, I haven't committed any crimes," wailed Hillman. "How can you think such things of me?"

"People don't get rich so quick, honestly," said Lee. "I'll tell you why you were willing to go on working for Mr. Dordress. You were afraid that if he learned how well fixed you were, he would take you out of his will."

"Well, yes, that's a fact," admitted Hillman. "It was natural, wasn't it?"

Lee's forefinger shot out. "Then you did know that you were down in Mr. Dordress' will."

Hillman's face turned ashy when he perceived the slip he had made. "I didn't so to speak know it," he stammered. "I only hoped that Mr. Dordress would remember me."

"Mr. Dordress was a younger man than you. In the natural course of things he would have outlived you."

Hillman was silent.

"Were you going to work on for him indefinitely on the chance of collecting your legacy?"

"I just didn't think the thing through, Mr. Mappin."

"I believe that you did think it through. I believe that you determined to make sure of your legacy before you gave up your job."

"No, sir! No, sir! No, sir!" cried Hillman frantically. "Such a thought never entered my head, Mr. Mappin! I won't touch a cent of the money now! I don't need it, anyhow. I have my own restaurant."

"The restaurant is entirely yours, then?"

"Yes. . . . No. . . . It will be! It will be!"

"Hillman," he said softly, "was the money for the restaurant or any part of it supplied by Miss Garrett?"

By Hillman's glance of panic Lee knew he had made a strike. "No, sir! No, sir! What for should Miss Garrett advance me money?"

"I'm asking you."

"No sir! Miss Garrett hasn't no use for me at all, Mr. Mappin. None whatever! Specially lately since I had orders from Mr. Dordress not to admit her to the apartment if he was there alone. I've had to take the rough side of Miss Garrett's tongue, sir. You have only to ask her what she thinks of me and you'll get an earful."

Lee studied him. He saw that he had Hillman badly worried, and determined to leave him in that condition. He got up, saying: "Are you coming to work tomorrow?"

"Why, certainly, Mr. Mappin. That is, if you want me."

"I want you."

"Then I'll be there, sir."

On his way home Lee telephoned Stan Oberry to assign a man to watch Hillman. "I don't think he's going to run for it; he's got too much at stake. However, let's not take any chances."

CHAPTER THIRTEEN

WHEN LEE GOT BACK to the Madison Avenue house he found Joe Dietz on duty in the elevator. "Joe," he said, "you have been shooting off your mouth too much about the death of Mr. Dordress."

"No, sir!" protested Joe. "I never said a word."

"Don't lie to me," said Lee. "I know."

Joe stared as if Lee had exhibited supernatural powers.

Up in the penthouse, Cynthia, hearing the door close, came out of her room in dressing-gown and slippers to meet him. Lee scolded her affectionately. She had a report that had been sent around from Stan Oberry's office earlier in the night, and she was curious to learn the contents. Lee read it aloud:

> "This morning when I was working out the lay of the Townley apartment in the Andorra, I saw that Mr. and Mrs. Townley's bedroom had two windows on the Sixty-sixth Street side of the building, and a third window opening on a court. A maid, in the apartment directly opposite, said she'd heard a woman scream across the court. She said a woman was having hysterics over there; kept crying out that somebody was dead and she would never see him again. There was a man in the room who was in a rage because the woman was carrying on so. The maid couldn't distinguish what he said, but she distinctly heard the woman cry out: 'You killed him! You killed

him! You murderer!' Apparently the man then left
the room, and the woman continued to have hyster-
ics on the bed. I haven't been able to approach any
of the Townley servants. Tappan, night doorman at
the Andorra, who gave me information this morning, has disappeared. I believe that Townley is taking care of him to keep him from talking further.

"A. A."

"Very questionable evidence," said Lee with a shrug. "It bears
no relation to what happened tonight. Gavin cannot have been
killed by two different people." He told her of the night's events.

"Another killing!" murmured Cynthia.

"This man was no loss," said Lee coolly. "I am sorry his mouth
was stopped only because he would have made a valuable witness."

Lee made hot drinks for Cynthia and himself to induce sleep.
While they sipped them in the studio he went over his case. One
by one, each suspect was considered. Hillman, Joe Dietz, Emmett
Gundy and Louella Kip. Siebert Ackroyd, Townley and his wife.
But nothing conclusive or satisfying came of it all.

When he undressed for bed, sleep was still far from Lee's eyes.
He was in Gavin's bare bedroom—Gavin favored Spartan simplic-
ity in his sleeping arrangements—and a sense of his lost friend was
strong with him; Gavin's droll smile; his rather slow and quizzical
manner of speaking; the suggestion of sadness in his eyes, though
he was the most serene of men and quick to laughter. Lee remembered his first sight of Gavin, a long-legged youth on the campus,
with eyes that saw what they looked at. For Lee, Gavin had never
changed; always the youth of twenty.

Realizing that he must have some sleep in order to cope with
the next day's work, Lee swallowed one of the barbital tablets that
he kept by him for such an emergency. He got into bed and slowly
sank into unconsciousness.

He found himself struggling from under a load of sleep with
terror in his heart. Something dreadful had penetrated to his
consciousness. He threw his legs out of bed and thrust his feet in

slippers. He ran out of his room and across the hall that separated him from Cynthia's room. Her door was open. He felt for the light switch and turned it. Her bed was empty. Running blindly through the corridor, he stumbled over her body lying on the floor of the foyer. He found the lights and, dropping beside her, gathered her in his arms.

She had fainted. She came to her sense in his arms and clung to him like a child. "Oh. Lee! There was somebody here!"

"Perhaps you had a dream," he said soothingly.

"No, Lee! I heard him. And then I saw him. I called for you, and then like a fool I fainted. I ought to have caught him and held him."

"Where was he?"

Cynthia pointed to the sunroom.

Lee, half believing it to be a hallucination, turned on lights in the sunroom. There lay a flower-pot smashed on the tile floor; the garden door was standing open.

"I had left my door open," Cynthia went on; "I heard something out in the middle of the apartment."

"Why didn't you call me then?"

"I thought I might be mistaken. I went out into the foyer. He was in the studio then. I could see the faint reflections of a flashlight in there. He came out. He had turned out his light. Just a shadow of a man. It was then that I called you. He dashed out through the sun-room. That's all I can remember."

Returning to his room, Lee threw on a warm dressing-gown, and snatched up gun and flashlight. Cynthia insisted on accompanying him into the garden, and he could not prevent her. The key to the garden door was hanging in its usual place beside the door frame. There was a second key sticking in the lock of the door. Lee took the key and closed the door so that the intruder could not slip back into the apartment while he was looking for him in the garden.

Ten minutes search satisfied him that the man was no longer there.

"Where could he have gone?" murmured Cynthia. "We are two hundred feet above the street."

"Either he flew away," said Lee dryly, "or he climbed the wall to the adjoining building. I favor the latter explanation."

They returned to the apartment. Any further sleep that night was out of the question.

"Could it have been Hillman?" suggested Cynthia.

"Hillman had the run of the apartment all day, and he's coming back in the morning. Why should he sneak in in the middle of the night?"

"No, it was not Hillman," she said. "A heavy, hulking figure, with stooped shoulders and a strange skull cap pulled close over his head." She shivered. "Somewhere I have seen such a figure, but I can't remember . . . I can't remember."

"What kind of a building is it next door?" said Lee. "I never happened to notice."

"An office building."

"It's four o'clock. Such a building would be locked up at this hour. I don't see how anybody could get in."

"Then what do you think?"

"I think that he had been waiting out in the garden all evening for a chance to come in. Perhaps he didn't know that anybody would be sleeping in the apartment tonight until he got on the roof and saw the lights."

Cynthia shivered. "He's been watching me all evening, then."

"My first job is to discover what he was after," said Lee. "Yesterday I made a complete mental inventory of the contents of the studio. I ought to be able to tell if anything has been taken."

Like an experienced hound Lee nosed about the big room, subjecting every inch of it to examination, while Cynthia, huddled in an easy-chair, watched him. The drawers of the big desk, the cupboards, the bookshelves, he omitted nothing. It was full daylight before he came to an end and threw up his hands in defeat. "Nothing is missing. So far as I can tell, everything in the room is exactly as it was yesterday."

Soon afterwards human arrived. He was calmer today; better able to meet their eyes. It was impossible to believe that he could have been the early-morning intruder.

When they had eaten breakfast Lee obstinately renewed his search of the studio. "The explanation *must* be here," he insisted.

In the end he came to Cynthia with a little ornamental wooden box in his hand. It contained a set of carved ivory chessmen.

"You have found something?" she said anxiously.

"Yes," he said, "but it only deepens the mystery. Gavin's set of chessmen has been taken away and another left in its place. The thief put the new ones in the old box. That's why I didn't discover the substitution before."

"The clicking of the pieces was the first sound that I heard," murmured Cynthia.

"These are similar to the others," Lee went on, "but the design of each piece is a little different. Notice that the castle is shorter and thicker through; the head of the knight more skillfully carved. I should never have discovered the substitution had I not been so familiar with the old set."

"It was the murderer!"

"So it would seem. Nobody else would have taken such a risk."

"What could he have wanted them for?"

"God knows, my dear! There is no mystery about Gavin's chessmen. He's had the set for twenty-five years. I remember well when he bought it. It cost fifteen dollars. That was a big sum for a college boy to lay out. Gavin was crazy about the game. He undertook to teach me, but I had not patience enough to make a good player. We will have to find the missing chessmen before we can hope to discover why they were taken."

CHAPTER FOURTEEN

WHEN HILLMAN next had occasion to enter the studio, the chessmen were lying exposed on a table. Cynthia watched the servant's face.

"Hillman, Mr. Dordress was a great chess-player, wasn't he?" asked Lee.

"Yes, sir," he answered readily. "Mr. Dordress was very partial to the game."

"With whom did he play?"

"Lately he had been complaining that he had nobody to play with, sir."

"And before that?"

"He used to play with Mr. Siebert Ackroyd, sir."

Cynthia paled.

"Mr. Ackroyd used to drop in evenings," Hillman went on. "Mr. Dordress said he had the makings of an A-1 player. But he hasn't been for some time past."

"Anybody else?" asked Lee.

"Miss Garrett, sir. Mr. Dordress taught her the game several years ago. I fancy she wasn't a very good player. Mr. Dordress would give her a handicap and then beat her. They used to play in the late afternoons or on Sunday evenings."

"Anybody else?"

"Not that I can recollect sir."

"Are these the chessmen that Mr. Dordress ordinarily played with?"

"Why yes, sir. He never owned but the one set."

"All right, thank you, Hillman. That's all now."

The servant cast a glance of sharp curiosity at the little ivory figures. "Excuse me, sir, but have you learned anything from these?"

"Nothing," said Lee.

When he had gone out Cynthia said: "The chessmen meant nothing to him."

"That is obvious," said Lee.

"Oh dear!" she complained, "everything we have learned today seems to cancel out everything we learned yesterday. Can you see any light?"

"A crack or two," he answered smiling. "It is possible that the principal in this affair employed several agents to carry out his plan . . ."

"Or her plan," murmured Cynthia.

"It has already been suggested that there were two such agents; there may have been more. Perhaps no one of these agents was informed of what the others were up to."

They went out into the roof garden to see what further clues daylight might reveal. A dull rumble of traffic arose from the street below, punctuated by the occasional squawk of a motor horn. Except for the evergreen hedges the garden wore the bleak dress of winter. The gravel paths revealed no trace of footsteps. In a broad box of earth outside the window of Cynthia's room Lee found the print of a big hand. It had been encased in a glove. "He was leaning forward here to peep between the slats of the Venetian blinds," said Lee.

Cynthia shivered.

Lee covered the hand print. Later in the day he took a cast of it with plaster of Paris. In order to reach the box the man had had to force his way through the growing evergreen. Lee, examining them through a magnifying glass, carefully collected some woolen hairs clinging to the spiny foliage.

All along the back of the garden ran the wall of the adjoining building, some fifteen feet higher than the garden. Gavin had covered it with a wooden lattice over which vines might be trained in summer. Lee said the man could not have climbed down and climbed back by the lattice. The interstices were too small to provide a toehold.

"Very likely he used a rope ladder," said Lee. "The supports of the tank on the roof next door would provide a convenient place to tie his ladder." Lee was presently able to point out the exact spot where the man had come down and gone back again. The painted lattice showed scuff marks. "The rope ladder," said Lee, "would have a tendency to throw him against the lattice, especially if he was in a hurry."

Back in the house, Lee put the hairs he had picked up under a microscope. After examination he said: "It was a cheap overcoat made of a material that contained wool and jute. Light brown or yellowish in color."

"A yellow overcoat!" murmured Cynthia, staring. "Now I remember, Lee. As I stood on the corner Sunday night a man wearing a strange-looking yellow overcoat passed me. He had a leather helmet drawn over his head. . . . Lee! . . . Lee! That was the man who broke in here last night. That was my father's murderer! . . . O God! Lee, he must have been on his way to kill him then!"

"Would you know him if you saw him?"

"O Heavens, yes! Every detail of his appearance seems to be etched on my brain!"

Lee, feeling that he had reached a point where he required the assistance of the police, drove down to Headquarters to talk to Inspector Loasby, the chief of the detective force. Cynthia went to her work at the New York Hospital. Lee's relations with the police were peculiar. On several occasions he had given Loasby valuable help, and the latter was presumably grateful. When a case broke Lee had always retired gracefully and let Loasby take the credit. The Inspector could not understand Lee's desire to be known as an author rather than a detective. Privately he considered Lee a bit cracked.

Loasby was a handsome man and a first-rate detective officer in the modern scientific manner. Perhaps he lacked something of imagination, but Lee considered that just as well in a public official. At Headquarters Lee found him and gave him the facts.

"Good God, Mappin, there's dynamite in this case! Gavin Dordress, Gail Garrett, Mack Townley, Bea Ellerman. What a bunch of headliners! We'll have to be damn careful before we move!"

"Are you telling me?" said Lee.

Loasby agreed that it would be better for the police to take no official cognizance of the case until Lee had secured more evidence. In the meantime Loasby put the resources of the department at Lee's disposal, and Lee on his part agreed to keep the Inspector fully informed.

Lee's first request was for a search to be made for the missing set of chessmen. Lee also handed the Inspector the key that he had found in the garden door of the penthouse. It was to be photographed and a circular printed and sent to every locksmith in the city with the object of learning who had made such a key.

Returning uptown, Lee visited the tall, narrow office building next door to the apartment house. Before making his presence known, he went up to the top floor, where he found a flight of stairs leading up. At the top was a door opening on the roof, furnished with an ordinary spring lock. By pressing down the catch on the lock, anybody could go out on the roof and return whenever he had a mind to. The roof offered no distinctive features. On the base of the iron standard supporting the water tank, Lee could distinguish marks where a rope or rope ladder had been tied.

He looked up the superintendent of the building. Posing as a private detective, Lee said: "The apartment of the late Mr. Dordress was entered last night. Apparently the thief lowered himself from the roof of your building."

"What did he get?"

"Nothing. He was scared off."

The superintendent told Lee that his building was kept open until 11:30 to suit the convenience of a school of Telegraphy on the top floor, which conducted classes every night of the week. There were two sessions, 7 to 9 and 9 to 11. The school was closed about 11:30 and the elevator man went home at the same time. Thereafter the outer door of the building was locked. There was a watchman who was required to visit every floor of the building four times between midnight and 8 A. M.

The superintendent admitted that it would be possible for anybody who was familiar with the movements of the watchman to slip past him on his rounds. In fact, the watchman had reported on Monday morning and again this morning (Tuesday) that he had found the front door of the building unlocked after he had locked it. For the coming night, a second man had been engaged to sit in the entrance hall while the other was making his rounds.

"He's hardly likely to come back again," said Lee dryly. "Best to say nothing about this for the present."

"You bet your life," said the superintendent. "I don't want any unfavorable publicity for my building."

The night elevator boy came on duty in the middle of the afternoon, and Lee returned later to talk to him. He was a keen boy, immediately interested when Lee questioned him. Feeling his way from question to question, Lee finally got this story out of him.

"Last Wednesday or Thursday—I can't be sure—I carried a funny-looking guy up to the Telegraph School. I marked him particular, he was such a dumb, foreign-looking cluck; most of the students up there are smart young American fellows. The first time he come he only stayed a few minutes and I took him down again. He came back Sunday night about a quarter to eleven. I told him the school would be closing in a few minutes, but he said he only wanted to register, and there was time enough for that. So I took him up."

"Did you bring him down again?" asked Lee.

"I didn't see him going down, but there's such a crowd when the school lets out I might easy miss seeing somebody. But I don't think I would have missed that funny-looking guy."

"Did you see him last night?"

"Yes. Last night he come in time for the nine-o'clock session."

"Did you carry him down again?"

"No, sir. Now that you ask me, I never saw him again. I forgot about him."

"Describe him."

"Well, he was a tall fellow and heavy-built; kind of stooped in the shoulders; almost like he had a hump on his back. I couldn't tell you the color of his eyes. He wore thick glasses that made his eyes funny-looking. He couldn't see very good; kind of felt his way along. Clean shaven. He was a Yiddisher. Talked broken. He had on a big overcoat kind of yellowish, that hung on him like a sack. You couldn't buy such an overcoat in this town. He musta brought it over from the other side. And a leather helmet; come right down over his head."

"Very good description," said Lee. "What age man?"

"I couldn't tell you, Mister. He wasn't young and he wasn't old."

"Would you know him again?"

"I sure would. . . . What's he wanted for, boss?"

"Trying to break into the apartment next door. . . . If you value your job say nothing about it."

CHAPTER FIFTEEN

LEE RETURNED TO THE APARTMENT. At the end of the day Stan Oberry sent around a batch of reports. There was nothing new on Mack Townley. He had slept at the Federal League Club. In the morning he had visited his apartment, and had then returned to the club, where he had remained hidden all day. Joe Dietz had, as usual, spent most of his day in the poolroom. He had refused to talk about the Dordress case today, and had appeared uneasy and suspicious. Gail Garrett had not left her apartment in the Conradi-Windermere all day. Stan's operative, Vosper, armed with a letter of introduction from Lee to the president, had visited the Farmers and Merchants Bank where Gail kept her account. Vosper had been furnished with some significant figures. On October 10th Miss Garrett's balance had stood at $18,000 and she had since made large weekly deposits. But she had drawn out no less than $25,000, paid to her personally in cash, $5,000 at a time; her present balance was less than $1,000.

There was nothing on Hillman, since he had been at work in the apartment all day. As a matter of fact, Schelling, who was assigned to watch him, had been detailed to discover what he could about the Harvest Restaurant on Jerome Park Avenue. Schelling reported that it was a small place doing an excellent business. Said to gross between twelve and fourteen hundred weekly, of which the net would be in the neighborhood of two hundred. It was efficiently managed by Mrs. Hillman, who spent long hours in the place, generally leaving between one and two in the morning. There

was such a person as Howard Harvest, and Hillman had undoubtedly bought the place from him. Hillman was said to have paid fifteen thousand for good will, fixtures, and lease. When Schelling
visited the address Hillman had given as Harvest's, he found that
the Harvests had moved some weeks before, giving out that they
were going to California.

Oberry at Lee's request had sent a man by plane to Reno, Nevada,
to get a statement from Mrs. Mack Townley.

In the afternoon paper Lee read that the body of Frank Cagey,
or Chigi, had been identified and removed from the Morgue. The
account stated that he was "lying in state" in the rooms of the Nonpareil Social Club, while his friends prepared a gangster's funeral
for him on a grand scale. Lee was relieved to see that no connection was suggested between the death of Gavin Dordress and the
killing of the burglar in the Bronx by Gavin's butler on the following night. The press commiserated with the unfortunate man who
had been concerned in two such tragedies.

When Cynthia came in from work, Lee laid all this before her.
When she had read the reports she said:

"It is now certain that Hillman has paid in full for his restaurant with money obtained from Gail Garrett."

"Fairly certain," agreed Lee cautiously. "I don't understand why
she paid Hillman so much since he does not seem to have taken
the principal part in the killing."

"What do you suppose she did with the other ten thousand?"

Lee shrugged. "I assume that Cagey got it."

At six o'clock a messenger came from Police Headquarters
bringing the missing set of chessmen. Loasby said that it had been
pledged early that morning in a pawnshop on Third Avenue. The
description of the man who had pawned it tallied with that furnished by the elevator boy, yellow overcoat, stooped back, and all.

"Nice work!" said Lee, sitting down to write the Inspector a note
of congratulation.

Lee set up the little red and white ivory chessmen on Gavin's
desk, and studied them piece by piece, both with the naked eye
and under a glass, while Cynthia awaited the verdict. For a long

time Lee was baffled; finally, as he studied one of the little castles with its battlemented top, an association of ideas began to work in his mind. From a drawer of the desk he got the little sketch he had made of the bruise on Gavin's forehead. Pressing the top of the castle in an inked pad that lay in Gavin's drawer, he made an impression of it on the paper alongside his own sketch. The two little pictures were identical; six tiny parallelograms ranged in a circle.

Cynthia stared at them with widening eyes. "Lee, you are wonderful!" she murmured.

"That tells the story," said Lee. "Gavin was playing chess with somebody at the moment he was shot. His head sank forward and struck against this chessman. I mentioned the bruise on Gavin's forehead to one of the reporters, and it was printed yesterday. That is what determined the murderer to make away with the telltale piece."

"Playing chess," murmured Cynthia . . . "with whom?"

"We know of three chess-players," said Lee grimly; "Gail Garrett, Jack Townley, and Siebert Ackroyd. There may have been others."

"It couldn't have been anybody but Gail," Cynthia said sharply. "Everything points to her."

"Everything but the man in the yellow overcoat," said Lee. "We haven't established any connection between him and Gail."

"We know that she has employed two accomplices. Why not a third?"

"That remains to be proven."

They heard the bell ring outside, and Hillman presently entered to say that Mr. Ackroyd was calling. He had asked for Miss Cynthia.

Cynthia's face was twisted with pain. "I won't see him," she said.

"Better take a look at him," Lee said to Cynthia in an undertone. "It may destroy your suspicion or confirm it."

Cynthia, after a painful hesitation, nodded her head.

"We'll come out to him," said Lee. He gathered up the chessmen.

Siebert was agitatedly pacing the foyer. His handsome face was drawn with anxiety. He was scarcely aware of Lee's presence. "Cyn, I had to come," he burst out. "I can't settle to anything when you're in such trouble. How goes it?"

Cynthia looked at him darkly. "All right," she said tonelessly. Evading his outstretched hand, she crossed the foyer to the opening of the corridor, and turning around, fixed him with her dark gaze. He was standing almost on the same spot where she had first seen the man who had entered the night before.

"What's the matter?" asked Siebert blankly.

Lee moved quickly towards the sunroom. "Come in here a moment, Siebert. I have something to show you."

Siebert strode into the sunroom, Cynthia watching every movement. Lee took down the key to the garden door from its hook on the door frame and showed it to him. "Siebert, did you ever borrow this key?"

Siebert's face showed purest surprise. "What are you getting at?" he demanded.

"I mean for the purpose of having a duplicate made," said Lee, watching him sternly.

Siebert flushed red with anger. "I don't understand you." Turning on his heel, the young man demanded of Cynthia, "What does this mean?"

Lee, who did not wish to be present during what followed, went back into the studio.

"What does this mean? What does this mean?" Siebert kept asking.

Cynthia, shrinking from him, mutely shook her head.

"Why do you act so strangely? You and Lee. It isn't possible that you suspect we of . . . *Me?*"

"You cursed him," she muttered.

Siebert clasped his hands to his head. "O my God!" he groaned. "Haven't I suffered enough on that account? I told you how sorry I was. It meant nothing. It was only the anger of a moment. . . . Cynthia, I have never hidden anything from you. You must know that I am incapable of such a thing!"

He paused, searching her face. Cynthia continued to look at him distantly, and his face suddenly flamed with anger. "All right!" he cried harshly. "I've given you the best I've got! Maybe you're not worth it. There must be something the matter with you, if you can so easily suspect the one who loves you. I reckon you're incapable of loving a man. If you loved me, you would know that I could not do this to you!" He strode out of the apartment.

Lee, hearing the door, came quickly back into the foyer. "Well?" he asked.

Cynthia ran to him with failing steps, and falling in his arms, burst into a passion of tears. "Lee, I don't know! I don't know!" she cried. "Sometimes I think it might have been Siebert; sometimes I am sure it was not! Why must I be tortured so? I can't bear it!"

"Have courage," he said, soothing her. "It won't be for long. We will soon know."

CHAPTER SIXTEEN

CYNTHIA AND LEE were seated at the dining-table. Cynthia pale, and with dark circles under her eyes, was merely playing with her food, and Lee couldn't eat because she couldn't. They heard the bell outside, and Cynthia looked up apprehensively.

"I dread that sound!" she murmured.

Hillman, having gone to the door, entered to say that it was Joe Dietz. He wanted to see Mr. Mappin. He said it was important. Lee got up and went out into the foyer, followed by Cynthia. The elevator boy in his street clothes stood there biting his lip and turning his hat ceaselessly between his hands. Joe was not a beauty at any time, and agitation made his sharp-featured face look even more common and mean.

"Mr. Mappin, I got to talk to you! I got to talk to you!" he stammered.

Hillman was hanging around, and Lee led the way into the studio. When the boy saw that Cynthia was coming, too, he hung back. "Mr. Mappin, I got to see you alone."

"Has it got anything to do with what happened Sunday night?" asked Lee.

"Yes, sir."

"Then she must hear it, too. Forget that she's a woman." Lee closed the door of the studio. "What is it, Joe?"

"Mr. Mappin, I lied to you yesterday morning."

"I suspected as much," said Lee dryly. "Give me the straight dope now."

"I lied when I said there was nobody come up to Mr. Dordress' apartment after everybody had gone. I brought up a man in the elevator."

"What man?" asked Lee sharply.

"Frank Cagey, Mr. Mappin. But I didn't know who he was then."

Lee and Cynthia looked at each other.

"There was a woman come to Mr. Dordress, too," stammered Joe.

"Who?"

"Miss Gail Garrett, sir."

Cynthia dropped suddenly into a chair as if her legs had weakened under her. "Now I *know!*" she murmured.

Lee said: "Sit down, Joe. Take it slow, and tell me the whole story."

"Yes, sir. Thank you, sir." Joe sat down on the edge of a chair, still turning his hat. "Mr. Hillman, he was the last to leave. Miss Garrett, she come back first. It was a good while after; about twelve, as near I can figure. She come back. She asked me if anybody had come to see Mr. Dordress, and I says no, and she seemed awful glad of it. She said: 'Take me up,' and I did."

"Did Mr. Dordress let her in?" asked Lee.

"No, sir. She had her own key to the apartment."

"You're sure of that?"

"Absolutely, Mr. Mappin. She was in such a hurry she had the key in her hand before she stepped out of the elevator, and she put it right in the door."

"Go ahead."

"I hadn't much more than got down to the ground floor when the fellow, he come. He was dressed so nice I never thought anything out of the way. He said he wanted to see Mr. Dordress, and that he was expected, so I took him up."

"Who let him in?"

"I don't know, sir. He rang the bell of the apartment. I couldn't hang around watching. I came down in the car."

"Then what happened?"

"Well, after a while I heard a buzz from the fifteenth floor and I went up to get them."

"How long were they in the apartment?" asked Lee. "This is important."

"I couldn't tell you exactly, Mr. Mappin. It was a good while. Not less than half an hour, and not more than an hour, I guess."

"Go on."

"The fellow he looked just the same as before, slick and smooth, but the lady, she looked bad. She was all in. He had to hold her up. I took them down in the elevator and they drove away in a taxi."

"Why did you lie about this yesterday?" asked Lee.

"Because I was scared, Mr. Mappin. In the elevator this fellow showed me a gun and said he'd fill my belly full of lead if I ever said that he or she had been there that night."

"Did he give you money?"

"No, sir. But she did. A hundred dollars. And promised me more if I kept my mouth shut."

"I see," said Lee.

"I didn't care nothing about the money, sir," protested Joe. "I'm an honest boy. Ain't I telling you the truth now? But I was *scared!*"

"What was it led you to tell the truth now?" asked Lee.

"I read in the paper as how Frank Cagey was shot up in the Bronx last night. The name meant nothing to me, but his picture was in the paper and I thought that was the guy. It said he was lying in state at — Bayard Street and I went there on my way to work. There was a crowd going in and out and nobody took no notice of me. I went in and looked at him in his casket, and it was the guy. So I wasn't scared of him any more. That's why I'm telling you."

"I see," said Lee.

"What must I do now?" asked Joe nervously. "Must I talk to the police?"

"All in good time," said Lee. "I'll tell you when. . . . In the meantime if you value your own skin keep your mouth shut. This fellow Frank Cagey has plenty of friends, remember."

Joe turned pale. "Yes, sir. You can depend upon me, sir."

"All right, go on to your work," said Lee.

When the boy had left them, Lee and Cynthia looked at each other for a long time without speaking.

"It's all clear now," murmured Cynthia at last. "Gail persuaded Dad to sit down to a game of chess with her, and this murderer stole up and shot him."

"So it would seem," said Lee. His voice lacked conviction. "I don't see why Gavin didn't take alarm when he first laid eyes on the man."

"He never laid eyes on him," said Cynthia. "Cagey only made believe to ring the doorbell. Gail had fixed the latch of the door so that he could go right in after the elevator had gone down."

"Maybe so," said Lee.

Cynthia reached for the telephone and began to dial a number. Lee, divining her intention, said quickly: "Better wait! We're not sure yet!"

Cynthia looked at him in astonishment. "What more proof could you want?"

"The man in the yellow overcoat was up here too on Sunday night. Where does he come in?"

"He was another of Gail's accomplices."

Cynthia got her connection. "Siebert," she said into the transmitter, and her voice broke; "Siebert, can you come over her for a moment? I have something to tell you."

Evidently Siebert could and would. Cynthia hung up.

"You were too precipitate," said Lee gravely.

"I can't help myself, Lee," she pleaded. "I wronged him in my mind!"

"What do you want me to do next?" asked Lee. "Lay the information before the police and ask for Gail Garrett's arrest?"

Cynthia looked at him in horror. "Oh, Lee! Think how the tabloids will play up the story of Gail and Dad!"

"I don't see how it can be avoided, my dear."

"Don't tell the police," she urged. "Let us just tell Gail that we know the truth, and leave her to her own conscience. That will be punishment enough."

Lee shook his head. "I have pledged my word to Inspector Loasby. It is my duty to tell the police everything we know. After that it's up to them."

"Must you tell them right away? Tonight?"

"Not tonight. I want to be surer of my ground first."

Hillman entered to ask if they would take any more dinner. Obviously it was only an excuse; his face was tormented with curiosity. They shook their heads, but he lingered. His curiosity proved to be stronger than his fears.

"Mr. Mappin, sir," he blurted out, "if it's not a liberty, what did you learn from the boy? What has happened?"

"Nothing conclusive," said Lee mildly.

"Mr. Mappin . . ."

"That will be all, Hillman."

The servant went out with a distracted air.

"Curious," murmured Lee, "the pertinacity of a weak man. Hillman will face this out to the end, though he dies a thousand deaths from sheer fright."

In ten minutes Siebert was at the door of the apartment. Cynthia ran out into the foyer; Lee remained sitting in the studio, mulling things over.

"Siebert," said Cynthia imploringly, "I'm sorry for the way I spoke and acted. Can you forgive me and forget it?"

The young man's eyes brooded over her somberly. "I forgive you," he said, "but I can't forget it right away. It made too deep a mark."

"I'm so sorry!" she murmured. "Try to put yourself in my place. Every hour something new happens. I am dragged this way and that. I scarcely know what I am doing."

"I know what you're going through," he said. "I wanted to stand by you. But you preferred Mr. Mappin."

"Why can't I have both of you?"

Siebert shook his head. "Mappin suspects me. Mind, I don't blame him for that. He's got to go by logic. But you ought to have known me better."

"You have not forgiven me," she said sadly.

"Yes, I have! I can't help loving you whatever you do." They drifted into the sunroom with linked arms.

As time passed and Hillman did not appear to say that he was going home, Lee went in search of him. He found the servant standing in the pantry in a distracted state.

"Haven't you finished your work?" asked Lee.

"Yes, sir. Quite finished."

"Then why don't you go home?"

"I was just going, sir." Hillman took his hat and coat from the cupboard where they hung. "Goodnight, Mr. Mappin. Please say goodnight to Miss Cynthia for me."

Lee made sure that he left the apartment.

Five minutes later Hillman was back again, shaking with fright. "Mr. Mappin, sir," he stuttered, "would it be all right with you if I stayed here tonight?"

"Why?" asked Lee.

"I believe there are men laying for me in the street, sir. Friends of that man . . . of Cagey's. If they don't get me here they are certain to get me in the empty streets that surround my home. I'm afraid."

"Nonsense!" said Lee. "When a thief is killed while breaking into a house it is a part of the chance he takes. You never heard of his friends trying to avenge a killing of that sort. It is only when a gangster is murdered by a rival that his mates look for revenge."

"I'm afraid," wailed Hillman.

"I see no reason for your staying here all night."

"I have a room, sir. Everything is prepared. I used to sleep here sometimes when Mr. Dordress was alive."

"No, Hillman."

"*Please!* Mr. Mappin."

"It does not suit my convenience to have you sleep here," said Lee.

Hillman shuffled away, fairly blubbering with fright.

The next morning Gavin's funeral took place. All of the man's closest friends attended the burial in Greenlawn Cemetery.

As the clergyman pronounced the benediction, Gail Garrett drew from beneath her coat a single white rose. She extended her graceful hand, matching the rose in whiteness, to drop it on the casket, but Cynthia was too quick for her. The girl's eyes blazed in her white face. Wrenching the flower from the other woman's hand, she cast it on the ground and trod on it.

"For shame!" she said in a low, quivering voice.

All the others looked on as if turned into stone. Gail shrank away. There was nothing theatrical in this gesture. "No! No!" she whispered. "You are wrong! I did not! I did not!"

"Go!" said the blazing Cynthia, pointing to the cars.

Gail turned and ran stumblingly to her car. Nobody else moved. She collapsed on her knees on the running-board, but contrived to get the door open, and to drag herself inside. The car sped out of the cemetery.

CHAPTER SEVENTEEN

ON HIS RETURN to town after the funeral, Lee went to Police Headquarters, where he put the whole story before Inspector Loasby. The Inspector was appalled by the task that lay before him. "Gail Garrett!" he exclaimed. "Good God! It is terrible to think of dragging down a name like that!"

Notwithstanding her demoralization at the cemetery, Gail was actually playing the matinee at the Greenwich Theatre. Lee had satisfied himself of that by telephone.

"She has courage," he remarked dryly.

"She must keep up appearances at any cost," suggested Loasby.

On matinee days it was Miss Garrett's custom to remain in her dressing-room between the two performances. She would have friends in to a light meal that she called "tea" and would afterwards sleep for an hour in preparation for the evening performance. Knowing this, Lee timed his call at the theater with Inspector Loasby for half-past six. He wanted to save Cynthia from the ugly scene, but she insisted on accompanying them. "My being there will break her down quicker than all the questions of the police," she said, and Lee submitted. Loasby was in plain clothes.

On their arrival at the stage door they were told that Miss Garrett's friends were still with her, and they sat down on property chairs behind the scenes to wait. Of the three the professional police officer was the most uneasy.

"I don't like this! I don't like this!" he kept muttering.

The star's dressing-room opened directly off the stage. Smiling, and apparently her usual self, Gail came to the door to say good-by to her friends, and she had, therefore, no excuse for refusing to see these other visitors. She silently stood away from the open door to allow them to enter. The room was furnished as a charming boudoir in the style of Louis Seize.

Gail's face changed at the sight of Cynthia. "You might at least have spared me this until to-morrow," she said bitterly. "I have another performance to go through with."

"If the people are not satisfied with your understudy, their money can be returned," said Lee bluntly. "Our business is more important than a missed performance."

"Who is this gentleman?" asked Gail.

"Inspector Loasby of the police."

All the color drained out of Gail's face. She ordered her maid, Catherine, to wait outside and to prevent anybody from entering. She led the others to an inner room which was furnished in more workmanlike fashion for the actual business of dressing and making-up. Feigning to be pushed for time, she threw a stained kimono over her negligee, and sat down in front of her mirror, letting her visitors find seats where they could. Thus she had her back to them. She drew on a cap to protect her hair, and commenced to dab cold cream on her face. The familiar occupation gave her courage.

"What do you want of me?" she asked in a strangled voice. The mirror was ringed with electric lights and the smeared face reflected in it no longer looked human.

In the presence of the great lady of the stage the embarrassed Inspector looked almost guilty himself. "I am sorry to have to say it," he muttered. "You are charged with the murder of Gavin Dordress."

She expected this, of course. Her busy hands trembled violently, but she attempted to laugh. "How perfectly ridiculous! Who makes such a charge?"

"Mr. Mappin."

Gail's agonized eyes were still fixed on her reflection in the mirror. Her pretense that she had to make ready for the stage was preposterous. "He has no basis for such a charge!" she said shrilly. "There is no evidence! There couldn't be!"

The Inspector looked at Lee. The latter said:

"When you left Gavin's place on Sunday night you drove home. Shortly afterwards you left the hotel again. You were driven to the Nonpareil Social Club in Bayard Street, where you sent in the driver to bring out a man known as Cagey or Frank Cagey, a notorious gangster with a reputation as a killer. You and Cagey drove away in another cab. About a half-hour later you turned up alone at Gavin's place. You were carried up in the elevator and let yourself into the apartment with a key. A minute or two later Cagey came and was admitted to the apartment. There are witnesses to swear to this. Nobody saw Gavin alive after that."

Gail sprang up from her chair and paced the little room, pressing clenched hands against her temples, a grotesque figure with her frenzied, white-daubed face. Cynthia turned away her head. Old habit was so strong that there was still something theatrical in all Gail's movements. "I did not kill him!" she cried. "I did not! I did not! But, O God! what a position I an in! How can I prove it! Only Cagey could save me, and he is dead!"

Lee was not at all moved by this display of emotion. "Quite!" he said.

"Do you deny that your movements on Sunday night were as Mr. Mappin has stated?" asked the Inspector.

"No!" she said. "That much is true. You have your witnesses, haven't you? But I did not kill him! I swear it!"

"You hired the man who fired the shot," said Lee.

"No! No! No!"

"How can you expect a jury to believe that?" asked the Inspector.

Gail came to a stand, pressing her head between her hands. "Listen! I'll tell you the whole story. You've got to believe me. . . . Listen! Listen! . . . It is true that I went mad on Sunday night. I loved Gavin Dordress and he cast me off in the most brutal and cold-blooded fashion! Me! Me!"

"That's a lie!" said Cynthia quickly. "My father could not . . ."

"Quiet!" murmured Lee. "What does it matter?"

Gail turned on him furiously. "Oh, it doesn't matter what *I* say!" she screamed. "I am nothing, I suppose. You always hated me, Lee Mappin . . ."

"Get on with your story," said Lee.

"He cast me off in the most brutal and cold-blooded fashion," Gail repeated, with a spiteful glance at the girl; "and I was mad! I could not endure such a load of shame and grief. I could not live in the same world with the man who had wronged me so. I knew this, man, Cagey—never mind how. I knew he would do what I wanted, for money. It's true that I went to him on Sunday night and gave him money to kill Gavin Dordress. I was mad . . . mad!"

Cynthia's eyes widened in horror. Lee moved closer to her.

"When I went home I wrote a letter to Gavin asking for a reconciliation," Gail continued, "and I gave that to Cagey to deliver. I knew that Gavin would read it, perhaps answer it, and Cagey was to shoot him then, and make his getaway. . . ."

Cynthia threw an arm over her face.

"But the moment Cagey left me a revulsion of feeling took place, and I was horrified at what I had done. I attempted to pursue him in another cab, but I lost him in the traffic. I offered my driver everything I had on me if he got to Gavin's place first, and we made it! We got there before Cagey did. Your witnesses told you that! I went upstairs to beg Gavin's forgiveness. The key?—I had possessed a key to his apartment for years. I let myself in. . . . O God! . . ." Gail's voice was choked by a dry-eyed hysterical sobbing.

"Go on!" said Lee sternly.

Holding her head, Gail dropped to her knees. "O God!" she moaned. Flinging herself at full length on the rug, she pounded on the floor with her clenched hands. "Gavin was dead!" she screamed. "Dead! Dead! . . . He lay in the studio with a hole in his temple and blood spreading on the floor. His body was still warm! O God! if I had only had the courage to kill myself then!"

Lee and the Inspector exchanged a glance. The former said: "Who killed him?"

Gail raised her convulsed face. "He killed himself! The gun lay where it had slipped from his hand. It was his gun. His letter of farewell was lying on the desk. . . . You know he killed himself! Could I have forged Gavin's handwriting? Or that ignorant brute Cagey? You have only taken advantage of appearances to bring this charge against me!"

"And then Cagey came," prompted Lee.

"He rang the bell," sobbed Gail. "I let him in because I was afraid to leave him standing there."

"And then?"

"I can scarcely tell you. We left together."

"But that was nearly an hour later. What were you doing during that time?"

"I was looking for my letters. I had written Gavin many letters; foolish, loving letters. I couldn't bear the thought of having them read by others."

"Did you find them?"

"No. Gavin must have destroyed them."

"Why did you pay Hillman such large sums of money?"

"I never gave Hillman a cent!"

"Then why did you send Cagey to Hillman's house?"

"I didn't send him there."

"That I am sure is a lie," said Lee.

"What do you think of the rest of the story, Mr. Mappin?" the Inspector asked, low-voiced.

"She is probably speaking the truth," said Lee. "It fits in with the other circumstances that I told you of."

Gail, amazed, partly raised herself, and started to scramble towards Lee's chair on her knees. "Oh, Lee! thank you for those words," she cried. "You are my friend. You will stand by me."

Lee sprang up with surprising swiftness, and backed away from his chair. "Don't touch me!" he said sternly. "You plotted to kill my friend!"

"But I repented!" she wailed, beating the floor. "I got there before Cagey. I am not guilty!" Seeing no mercy in Lee's face, she collapsed, shaken by dry sobs.

CHAPTER EIGHTEEN

AT THIS POINT in the investigation, Lee Mappin, after consultation with Cynthia and Inspector Loasby, changed his tactics.

Suspecting that the real murderer of Gavin Dordress was close enough to them to be able to inform himself of all their movements, Lee undertook to lull him into a false security by making believe to drop the investigation. On the day following the scene in the Greenwich Theatre, therefore, Lee and Cynthia returned to their respective apartments; Gavin's personal effects were stored, and the penthouse subleased to an oilman who had made a strike in the Southwest and had come to New York to spend his gains.

The interest of the press in the case ceased with the funeral. Word was dropped in the proper quarters among Gavin's friends that there had seemed to be suspicious circumstances surrounding his death, but that Lee Mappin, after making an investigation, was satisfied that it was a case of suicide. Young Alan Talbert was the principal medium used by Lee to circulate this story. Talbert was a playwright of mediocre talents who was still among the great unproduced, but he was a lively, talkative young fellow and an assiduous frequenter of theatrical parties.

In order to cover his tracks more completely, Lee did for a while abstain from making any moves in the case. Stan Oberry was paid off, and his operatives recalled from their assignments. The man sent to Reno had not been able to get anything out of Bea Townley. When Lee started cautiously to put out new lines, he employed other agents and changed them frequently. Meanwhile he resumed his ordinary unhurried life, devoting himself to his writing and showing himself freely in public. He cultivated the society of Alan Talbert at this time. He did not care particularly for that shallow young man, but Talbert was flattered at being taken up by the noted Lee Mappin, and Lee was thus sure that his doings would be reported in the right places.

During these days Lee and Cynthia avoided private meetings. The telephone was safer. When they had first laid their plans Cynthia expressed a wish to take Siebert Ackroyd into the secret.

"I can't play a part with Siebert," she said.

Lee's face, usually so gentle to Cynthia, turned hard. "Not with my consent," he said. "Wait until I have cleared him of all possible suspicion."

"Very well," she said sadly. "Then I won't see him at all."

"Just as you think best."

Siebert was not the man to take this tamely. After Cynthia had put him off a couple of times, he flew into a rage and swore that he was through. Thereafter they heard reports that he was drinking too much and otherwise living recklessly, and that made Cynthia sore. She tried to lose herself in her work at the hospital and to put Siebert out of her life for good.

With the disappearance of Siebert, Emmett Gundy began to constitute himself Cynthia's squire. Cynthia was a rich woman now. Emmett aimed only to be the faithful friend, never obtruding himself, but always at hand when wanted. His daily calls on the phone to see how she was, his little inexpensive gifts, lapped her in kindness. Little by little she overcame her initial dislike of her father's classmate. They talked much of Gavin. There was no envy in Emmett now. One day Emmett and Siebert met accidentally in the anteroom of a publisher's office. There were no witnesses to what happened, but Emmett suffered a black eye. This had the result of further angering Cynthia against Siebert and making her kinder to Emmett.

Louella Kip no longer appeared at the little gatherings of their circle, and Emmett, when questioned, said that he had not seen her lately. Lee, becoming anxious, looked her up. He found her absolutely without means, about to be evicted from her cheap boarding-house, and with no place to go. She was still defiantly loyal to Emmett and would hear no word against him. In spite of her protests, Lee took care of her financially, and through theatrical connections of Gavin's,—not Mack Townley—succeeded in getting her a small part in a new play.

Gail Garrett continued to appear in "White Orchids" at the Greenwich, but it was obvious that she had lost her grip. Audiences are very quick to sense that sort of thing. Business fell away with startling rapidity; the play closed, and for the first time in many years the famous actress found herself "at liberty." She was no longer seen around her former haunts. In order to account for her failure, people began to say that she was taking drugs.

Hillman, when he was relieved of his duties as butler, disappeared from view. Mrs. Hillman was still doing an excellent business at the Harvest Restaurant, and Lee having learned that she was in communication with her husband, let Hillman go for the moment, satisfied that he could lay hands on him at any time. After a week or two had passed, Hillman returned to town and took up his duties in the restaurant. Inspector Loasby kept him under surveillance.

In the course of time the police were able to produce the man who had made the duplicate key to the garden door of the penthouse. It was a Jewish locksmith from the lower East Side. His description of his customer tallied with that already in the hands of the police: a tall, heavy-built foreigner with stooped shoulders. Wore thick glasses that caused him to peer in an odd way, and spoke broken English. The Jew, however, insisted that he was a Wop. Wore a leather cap that completely covered his hair, and an old yellowish overcoat that had sagged out of shape. The various people who had seen this man could not agree as to the color of his eyes. One said black, one said grey, one said blue. This description had been put in the hands of every policeman in New York.

EARLY IN NOVEMBER there was an announcement in the dramatic columns of the New York dailies that Mack Townley had discovered a remarkable new playwright. His name was John Venner and he had written a play called "Sin," which was so good that the astute Townley had bought it on sight and was preparing to put it into rehearsal as soon as a cast could be assembled.

Every few days thereafter the public was fed an additional bit of news about the new play. There was a mystery about the author. Mack Townley had not laid eyes on him. All their business had been conducted by correspondence. The Townley office declined to give out his address. Though this was presumably Venner's first play, he had had the assurance to stipulate that no changes should be made in it, and Townley had actually agreed.

Very little about the play itself was given out in advance. It was said to deal with a strange case of the transference of personality, and while not a horror play in the usual sense, to have breath-taking overtones of terror and mystery. Another account described it as an allegory in modern dress.

It was soon announced that the cast had been completed and rehearsals started. The play was to open at the Townley Theatre on Christmas night. It would have one of the most expensive casts ever brought together. The principal woman's part would be played by Miss Beatrice Ellerman (Mrs. Mack Townley), who had recovered from her recent illness.

Lee smiled grimly as he read this last item. Bea was back in town. The fact of her brief stay in Reno had not been published in the press, and nobody but Lee and his close associates knew that the couple had separated and come together again. One morning Lee met Bea coming out of the most fashionable beauty salon on the Avenue. The tall Bea in her dark slenderness and grace was more dazzlingly beautiful than ever. Everybody on the sidewalk turned to look at her. She moved across, smilingly conscious of her power. Her greeting to Lee was nicely graduated between pleasure at the sight of an old friend and grief at the recollection of their common loss.

"Why on earth did you send that person all the way to Reno to ask me questions?" she asked.

"Well, there were certain suspicious circumstances in connection with Gavin's death, but they are cleared up now."

"But why question *me?*"

Lee smiled his blandest smile, "My dear, you were overheard applying very uncomplimentary epithets to your husband. In fact, you called him . . . a murderer."

Bea paled under her make-up and bit the deliciously painted lip. "Lee! Who said so?"

"A servant."

"Maybe I did," she murmured. "But a woman out of her mind with grief and hysteria—it means nothing."

"Quite!" said Lee.

He handed her into her car. Driving away, she did not look quite so sure of herself.

Several nights later Lee saw Mack Townley at the annual dinner of the Pilgrims. Mack, who had large interests in London as well as New York, was at the speakers' table. Lee marveled at the transformation in him. Gone was the savage look of pain and defeat. Mack had returned to his usual smooth and astute self; the handsomest and the best-dressed theatrical manager of two continents. His speech in the prevailing hands-across-the-sea vein was the wittiest of the evening. Mack had not written it himself, of course, but he delivered it admirably. Lee did not run into him until the party was breaking up.

"Hello, Mack!"

"Well, Lee!" said Mack coolly; he was never a demonstrative man. "How are things going?"

"As usual. I hear great tales about your new play."

Mack became the promoter at once. "In this case, Lee," he said seriously, "the ballyhoo is not exaggerated. It is really an extraordinary play. I have never seen actors so deeply affected by their parts. The play inspires them."

"Splendid!" said Lee.

"You shall have two tickets for the opening," said Mack, hurrying away.

"Thanks, old man."

As the date of the opening approached, the contention for tickets became intense. Any Mack Townley opening was an event in New York's social year, and this was considered to be exceptional.

From the *Herald Tribune* of December 20th: "Two seats for the opening of 'Sin' at the Townley Theatre on Christmas night were sent to the author, the mysterious Mr. John Venner, in the usual course. The astonishment of the management can be better imagined than described when they were returned yesterday with a note from Mr. Venner stating that he did not expect to attend! An author not coming to the first night of his first play! Incredible! However, upon thinking it over, one realizes that if Mr. Venner had occupied the numbered seats sent to him he would immediately have been identified. No doubt he will be present, but in a place of his own choosing."

Lee Mappin received his tickets in due course. He called up Cynthia to ask her if she would go with him.

"Thanks, dear," said Cynthia, "but I haven't seen a show since—well, you know when. I have a sort of dread of entering a theater. Ask somebody else to go with you."

"My dear, this is weak-minded," protested Lee. "The sooner you overcome it the better. Gavin wouldn't have liked to hear you speak like that."

"Perhaps you're right," she said. "Very well, I'll go."

CHAPTER NINETEEN

WHEN LEE MAPPIN'S CAB came to a stop in front of the Townley Theatre, the sidewalk was jammed from curb to wall with a pushing
throng of people, craning their necks to get a glimpse of the arrivals.

Inside the theater they saw Emmett Gundy at a distance, but
he was unable to reach their sides because of the crowd; and Alan
Talbert, beautifully arrayed, who prided himself on knowing
everybody. On the other side of the house rose the handsome head
of Siebert Ackroyd inches above the surrounding heads. He was
accompanied by a flamboyant girl who was determined to be looked
at. Cynthia looked once and not again.

The curtain was late, as usual. Every place in the house was
occupied except the two stage boxes. At the last moment a woman
entered the box on the left, but sat so far back behind the curtain
that they could see only her silken knees. Something in the house
below attracted her attention; she leaned forward and they had a
glimpse of Gail Garrett's drawn, white face. After the curtain had
risen, Mack Townley and several of the members of his staff quietly entered the box on their right.

The play opened very quietly. The setting represented the living-
room of a somewhat dilapidated Maryland manor-house, with tall
windows open to the summer night. There was a scene between a
middle-aged man and a handsome youth, his adopted son. They
were deeply attached to each other. The boy was leaving home to
be married. Lee approved of the play from the start; an atmosphere

was created; tender, charming, yet faintly portentous. He glanced at Cynthia to see how she was taking it, and was surprised to find her leaning forward with parted lips, drinking in every word. So far as he could see, nothing had happened on the stage to account for such excitement.

From time to time he glanced at her. Her excitement increased. She had lost herself completely. An intensity had come into her gaze at the stage that was almost like pain. Her hands were gripping the arms of her seat. Lee became very uneasy.

When the curtain fell on the first act there was a buzz of comment through the house; very little applause. The sophisticated first-night audience saves that for the end. When the lights went up Cynthia seemed to experience a slight collapse. She went limp all over and her head dropped. She then looked around her in a slightly shamed manner to see if her emotion had been noticed.

"Like it?" asked Lee casually.

"No! . . . Yes! . . . I don't know," she answered uncertainly. "But of course I liked it!" she went on a little feverishly. "It's wonderful! It did things to me. It frightens me a little. As if . . . as if . . . how can I explain it? as if it was written by somebody who knew too much about me? It was like echoes out of my own past."

Lee patted her hand. He thought her language overstrained.

In the intermission many of the people got up to join the crush at the back, in order to see or to be seen, but Lee and Cynthia remained in their comfortable seats. Out of the tail of his eye Lee saw Siebert Ackroyd striding up the aisle. Siebert cast a savage glance at Cynthia. They had several visitors, including the good-looking Alan Talbert, who, while he was talking, looked all around to see who was noticing him. He was excited about the play.

"A smash hit!" he cried.

"Isn't it a little too soon to tell?" suggested Lee.

"No, sir! You can feel it in the air. And Mack Townley is too wily to give them a first act that is not held up by what follows. Tomorrow morning the author will be famous."

"Does anybody know anything about him?" asked Cynthia softly.

"No. I happen to know that that's not just press-agent stuff. Up to now he has really kept under cover. But you can depend on it he'll appear as soon as he knows he has a hit on his hands."

In the second act the tension increased as the audience perceived the devilish net that was spread for the hapless youth. The men were more important than the women in this play, and it was not until the second scene of the second act that Bea Ellerman made her appearance. She took the part of a young girl, the youth's *fiancée*. Her perplexity and dismay at the subtle change that had come over her lover were touching in the extreme. Cynthia was breathing fast and her face had become agonized as she watched the scene. Lee touched her arm.

"My dear, it's only a play," he whispered.

She turned her strained eyes on him, dark and enormous. "Can't you hear it?" she whispered.

"Hear what?"

"My father's voice."

He stared at her, too startled to speak.

"This is Dad's play, Lee."

"No! No!" he whispered. "It's only your fancy."

She obstinately shook her head. "He is speaking to me through all the lines of the play. These are his thoughts, his feelings, his very words! That is what moves me so!"

Lee, gazing in her face, half believed it. He was a logical man, but he knew there was that in the human consciousness which transcends logic. Pressing her hand, he whispered: "Get a grip on yourself! Draw a mask over your face. If you are right, it is certain that the thief who stole Gavin's play is watching us now."

"I'll try," she whispered.

A revolving stage had been installed for the production of "Sin," and in each act the scenes succeeded each other without any pause. In the third scene of the second act the wrecked youth, robbed of everything that makes life worth living, crawled home to his foster-father's house. The recognition was heart-breaking. Cynthia's shoulders were shaking.

"Lee, I've got to go," she whispered. "I can't bear any more!"

"But if you go the guilty one will know that we have discovered his guilt," he protested.

"If I stay he will see it in my face when the lights go up. I cannot hide it!"

Fearful that she might break down in the middle of a scene, he hurried her up the aisle. As they passed through the lobby the curtain fell on the second act and they heard the audience, forgetting its sophisticated nonchalance, break into wild applause.

"You go back," whispered Cynthia. "You might learn something."

"I won't leave you," he said.

In the cab Cynthia broke down completely. He held her close. "Oh, what a relief to get away from people," she wept. "I'm sorry you were disappointed in me, but I couldn't stand any more!"

"It's no matter," said Lee.

"Lee," she said, "that man in the play felt towards his boy just as my father felt towards me. My father talked to me in just that way. Hiding his deepest feelings under a joke!"

"That may be a coincidence," said Lee.

"No! No! There are too many coincidences! . . . Listen! My father lived in New York for so many years that everybody has forgotten he was raised in Tidewater Virginia. There were a hundred references to Virginia. It's true they called it Maryland in the play, but that was just a stall. The scent of the wild grape flower in June—notice the word scent, Lee; anybody but Dad would have said perfume—the song of the mocking-bird; the haze that broods on the Chesapeake in summer; the trumpet-flowers and the wild black-berries in the hedges; the buzzards wheeling against the blue!"

"Anybody who knew Virginia might speak of these things," said Lee.

"All right. Take the peculiar sense in which he used the word spontaneity. My father loved that quality and that word. You must have noticed it. And the word inveigle used in place of intrigue. Besides many others of his pet words. And his speaking of how a good man was always at a disadvantage in the presence of a wicked man. Can't you see his smile when he said it? Lee, if I had the script of the play before me I believe I could point out all the places where some clumsy hand has changed and cheapened it! Think of the title; the right name of that play is 'The Changeling'; 'Sin' is a vulgar substitution!"

"You need go no further," said Lee. "I am convinced.

"When we find John Venner," he said presently, "we will have Gavin's murderer."

CHAPTER TWENTY

As ALAN TALBERT had foretold, the name of John Venner was famous in New York next day. All the newspapers joined in lavishing praises on his play.

The success of the play in connection with the non-appearance of the author warranted a news story in most of the papers, in addition to the dramatic review. It was told how Mack Townley, the producer, had sent Venner a telegram after every act, but had received no word in reply. However, Mr. Townley was giving a party in his apartment after the performance tomorrow night, for the "Sin" company, the gentlemen of the press and his friends generally, and he fully expected the mysterious John Venner to be present.

Cynthia Dordress, busy at her desk in the hospital, was surprised to hear the voice of Mack Townley over the wire at noon. The great man rarely condescended to use the phone. Having had time to gather her forces, Cynthia answered him calmly.

"How are you, my dear?" asked Mack.

"Quite well, thanks."

"Somebody told me that you were forced to leave the theater in the middle of the show last night."

"Yes. Wasn't it silly of me to be taken sick at such a moment? The worst of it was, it made Lee miss the play, too. I was all right an hour afterwards, and I'm anxious to go again as soon as possible."

"How about tomorrow night?"

"I'd love it, if it's convenient."

"Surely! You'll find two seats waiting for you at the box-office."

"Thanks so much. I'll try to get Lee."

"Afterwards perhaps you'll both come to our apartment. Bea and I are giving a little shindig at midnight. We hope to have the mysterious John Venner on view, but can promise nothing."

"How kind!" said Cynthia, "but I don't feel that I have any business amongst all the celebrities!"

"What!" said Mack, " the daughter of my oldest friend who was the greatest light of the American stage! What nonsense! Come, and uphold the name of Dordress, my dear."

"Very well," said Cynthia, "and thank you."

She immediately called up Lee and repeated her conversation with Mack. "What do you think of it?" she asked anxiously.

"Hum!" said Lee. "I prefer not to say over the phone."

"Well, we can talk about it later."

"Do you really feel able to sit through the play again?"

"Surely. I am braced for it now. I must see this play through. It was the shock of discovery that upset me last night."

"And the party afterwards?"

"Surely."

"He won't come," said Lee.

"He might," said Cynthia.

Cynthia sat through the third performance of "Sin" without an outward tremor. "It gives me pleasure now," she said to Lee. "It's a beautiful play. It is only the changes in it that anger me. I'd like to see it every night."

Lee pressed her hand.

"Do you think it was Mack Townley who stole it?" she asked coolly.

"I'm not prepared to say," growled Lee. "If he had, it would have been like him to call you up yesterday. Mack plays poker. But give me a little more time."

MACK AND BEA TOWNLEY welcomed their guests at the door of their big living-room. Bea, in white-and-gold brocade with her diamonds

and emeralds, looked queenly; but Lee, glancing from one woman
to another, considered that Cynthia's white skin and pure profile,
set off by a dull black evening gown, was the more beautiful. Bea,
pressing Cynthia's hand between both of hers, murmured:

"Darling, I'm so glad you could come. They told me you were ill."

"I was better in an hour," said Cynthia.

"Do come some day when we can have a little time together."

"I work in the daytime," said Cynthia, smiling; "some Sunday,
perhaps."

"Good! I'll give you a ring."

Lee listened to this with a dry expression. Both women were
lying, and each knew it.

Mack's handsome hard face wore its customary mask of scorn-
ful good humor. His courtesy was perfect.

The living-room was sixty feet long, and with the library at one
end and a great dining-room opening at the side, the suite could
accommodate two hundred people without crowding. Pink roses
were banked between the windows. All the luminaries of New York
professional and café society were present—millionaires, actresses,
divorcees, playboys, and titles. The most popular persons present were
the social commentators and press photographers, who were hailed
with cries of welcome as they circulated with notebook and camera.

"Such is modern society," grumbled Lee.

Everybody was eating lobster salad and drinking champagne.
Each plate had a little rack affixed to the rim to hold a glass, so
that two-handed creatures could accomplish this feat while standing. Waiters threaded their way through the throng, filling the
glasses as fast as they were emptied. A deafening clatter of conversation filled the rooms.

As Cynthia and Lee slowly made their way through, they met
many acquaintances. Gail Garrett appeared to be the only member of Gavin Dordress' old circle who was not present. Emmett
Gundy attached himself to them. Emmett did not appear to advantage in the brightly-lighted room. The thinning hair on his crown
was painfully apparent, his face was sourer and more pinched than
usual. He said to Cynthia:

"Disgusting mob! I'm surprised that you cared to come."

"Oh, once in a while it's amusing," she answered.

Alan Talbert came up to them pale and glassy-eyed with excitement. "Glorious occasion!" he said. "Drink with me. I'm on the threshold of a new life!"

At the moment his words didn't seem to make sense. "It's the champagne," muttered Emmett as they passed on.

They came face to face with Siebert Ackroyd in the dining-room doorway. Emmett paled and edged aside. Siebert, ignoring both Emmett and Lee, fixed his eyes on Cynthia with an expression both savage and full of pain.

"You look handsome," he said to her.

"Same to you," said Cynthia, coolly meeting his glance.

"I'm glad to see you coming out of your shell," said Siebert, "but I don't like your company."

"I do," said Cynthia smiling and moving on.

Later, Lee and Cynthia were standing against the wall of the big room, watching the tail-coated men and the bejeweled women weaving and clustering in front of them. The noise had grown louder; one had to shout to make oneself heard. The free champagne had been downed too quickly, and many of the faces seemed to have softened like butter in a warm room. Cynthia said in Lee's ear:

"I wish we lived in the country."

"I get you, my dear."

There had been no new arrivals in some time, and Mack Townley was now circulating through the room, pausing to say the right word to everybody. He said to Lee:

"I'm looking around for an unexplained person who might be the playwright. But I seem to know everybody here."

Lee said, when Mack had passed on, "If he's bluffing, it's well done!"

Mack finally climbed on a chair at the end of the room and clapped his hands to command attention. "Friends, Romans, Countrymen," he said smilingly, "I am sorry to say that I cannot produce my playwright. What has happened to him I don't know. I

am unable to picture an author who could pass up such an opportunity to receive the homage of the cream of New York. It may be
that . . ."

"Wait a minute, Mack!" cried a voice below him. "He's here!"

An excited murmur passed through the crowd. There was a
craning of necks. They saw Alan Talbert pushing up to Mack's chair.
"In me you see John Venner," he cried, striking a mock attitude.

There was an astonished silence, followed by a burst of applause. Everybody pushed up towards the chair, leaving Lee and
Cynthia on the outskirts of the crowd. Mack looked a little taken
aback, but he smiled still. He stepped down from the chair, and
Talbert, without waiting to be asked, climbed upon it and turned
his white face and punch-drunk eyes on the crowd.

"I am the author of 'Sin,' God forgive me," he announced. "I
wrote it on my little Corona!"

There was a tremendous burst of handclapping in which Mack
Townley, always the diplomatist, joined. On the outskirts of the
crowd Cynthia's eyes fired up dangerously, and Lee could almost
see the words shaping on her lips, "You lie!" He pressed her hand.

"Quiet!" he whispered. "This is not the place."

Cynthia relaxed.

"I got tired of rushing my plays around to the managers' offices and having them fired back at me with insincere praises,"
Talbert was saying. "You all know what people say about me; 'Alan
Talbert? Sure! Nice lad, but he can't write for a damn!' That was
my label. When you get a label it's useless to struggle. So when a
real bang-up, number-one idea for a play came to me I said nothing about it. And when it was finished I invented this John Venner
in order to get a fresh hearing. And as it has turned out I seem to
have been justified. . . ."

More applause.

"Lee, that is the man!" murmured Cynthia.

"I am not convinced of it," said Lee.

She looked at him in surprise. "He could have done it, Lee. He
was a frequent visitor at Dad's place. He is tall enough to have worn

the yellow overcoat. He had plenty of opportunities to steal the key to the garden door and have a duplicate made."

"Sure," said Lee. "But think it over. If he had stolen the play he would have been watching you the first night. When he saw you leave the theater he would have known you suspected something. He would never have had the courage to stand up and claim the play to your face tonight."

"But he *has* claimed it."

"There is a possibility that when the author failed to turn up tonight, Talbert figured that he never would acknowledge his play. So Talbert may have decided to claim the credit. Even though the deception is quickly discovered, Talbert will have had his day in the news."

"Let's get out of this," whispered Cynthia.

As they were making their way through the foyer, they saw Mack, suave, smiling, never at a loss, dealing with a knot of reporters.

"Do you believe in this claim of Alan Talbert's?" one asked him bluntly.

"Certainly I believe in it," said Mack. "Talbert is a friend of mine."

"Has his work in the past shown the promise that would justify you in thinking he wrote 'Sin'?"

"I don't know. I haven't read his other plays."

"Won't you require him to present documentary proof of the authorship of 'Sin'?"

"No," said Mack with an air of surprise. "Why should I?"

"Well, there's the question of paying the royalties."

"That doesn't concern me," said Mack. "The play was sent me by an agent. I pay the royalties to the agent. It's up to him to decide who they belong to."

"Who is the agent?"

"Siebert Ackroyd. He's here somewhere."

Cynthia's grasp of Lee's arm tightened painfully. "Oh, let's get away! " she whispered.

CHAPTER TWENTY-ONE

THE STORY OF WHAT HAPPENED at Mack Townley's party broke too late to make the morning papers. Lee had to wait for the first afternoon editions which came out in the middle of the morning. In addition to what Mack had told the reporters, Alan Talbert had given out a flamboyant interview in which he described how he had written "Sin"; and Siebert Ackroyd, talking more cautiously, told how the play had come to him by mail with a covering letter. He had had a number of letters from the author since, but had never laid eyes on the man. He had transmitted the advance payment by post-office money order, according to the author's instructions. He refused to give the author's address. As to Alan Talbert, Siebert said he saw no reason to question his claim, but that, of course, as a business man, he must await legal proof before paying him any royalties.

Subsequent editions of the papers described how busily Mr. Alan Talbert was making hay while the sun shone. He displayed no reluctance to talk to the press. Before the day was out he had sold options on two of his earlier plays to other New York producers, and had banked the advance payments. These producers stipulated that the plays must be billed with the name of John Venner as author, to which Talbert had cheerfully agreed. Talbert had signed a contract to go to Hollywood later at a handsome salary, and in the meantime had accepted a radio engagement. The Hollywood producers were bidding against each other for the rights of "Sin."

129

Meanwhile, from early morning, Lee, leaving Siebert Ackroyd aside for the moment, had been checking up on his office force. Siebert employed five persons; a secretary, a woman assistant, a male office manager, a second stenographer, and a messenger to tote manuscripts around. Lee, from amongst his wide connections, chose operatives here and there, and assigned one to make contact with each of the Ackroyd employees. It was the stenographer who proved to be the weak sister. She fell hard for the lively and attractive young man who was put on her trail, and by one o'clock on Friday morning (the Townley party was on Wednesday night) Lee was in possession of all the gossip of the Ackroyd office concerning their mysterious client, John Venner. The story was as follows:

The original script of "Sin" as received by Siebert Ackroyd had been typed on an old machine with a worn ribbon. This had occasioned a good deal of ill temper in those who read it, because of the eye-strain involved. It contained many typographical errors which had been laboriously corrected on the machine. Thus the author's handwriting appeared nowhere in the script. The arrangement of speeches, business, etc., indicated that the author was not familiar with the customary way of preparing a playscript. The agency's first act was to have some fair copies typed. The original script was filed. The letter which accompanied the script had been typed on the same machine, but it was signed by hand with a scrawly and imperfectly formed signature which looked as if it might be that of a very old man. Subsequent letters were all signed in the same way. For an address they gave a post-office box in Newark, New Jersey.

The latest letter from "John Venner" had been received on Wednesday. This one bore no address at the top. The writer implied that he had seen the first performance of "Sin" the previous night, but showed no pleasure at its success. He was writing, he said, to inform his agent that he was "traveling," and to instruct him to hold all communications, remittances, etc., until further notice. Obviously he had not traveled far, because the envelope bore the postmark of Stamford, Connecticut, which is only thirty miles from New York. He enclosed a power of attorney to enable Siebert Ackroyd to act for him in all ways.

Lee immediately had a watch put on the Newark post-office box, but it was never visited again. Siebert Ackroyd's last letter to his client lay in it unclaimed. Clearly, John Venner had taken alarm.

The Ackroyd office received another letter from him on Friday, angrily repudiating Alan Talbert's claim to the play. Venner undertook to prove that he had written the original script by describing the errors and corrections on a certain page. He suggested that Siebert should invite Alan Talbert to submit to a similar test. Venner said that he had a carbon copy of the script in his possession which he would produce "at the proper time."

Siebert sent copies of this letter to the press and it was printed in the afternoon editions. Thus, after twenty-four hours of sunshine, young Mr. Talbert went into eclipse. But not altogether. He had made the headlines; his name had become news. Once a name is news, New Yorkers are prone to forget how it first got that way.

On Friday night after dinner, Lee, Cynthia, and Fanny Parran were discussing these things in Lee's apartment. Cynthia's eyes were dark with pain. She said with extreme bitterness:

"It was Siebert. That is clear."

"Nothing is proved," said Lee.

Cynthia shook her head impatiently. "Don't try to soften the blow. I've got to take it. It was Siebert. The power of attorney proves it. John Venner will never be heard of again. Siebert will collect the royalties under his power of attorney. I will never believe in anybody again."

"It might just as well have been Mack Townley," insisted Lee. "Venner's stipulation that the play must first be offered to Townley suggests that."

"Mack is a business man," said Cynthia. "You know he wouldn't hand over a fortune in royalties and movie rights just for a gesture."

"He might think that it was worth it for the sake of diverting suspicion from himself."

Cynthia shook her head again. "What's the next move?" she asked.

"I will have them put under surveillance," said Lee. "I will have a look at Venner's letters and at the original script."

"How will you go about that?"

He smiled at her.

Cynthia was still in his apartment when there was a ring at the door and a package was handed in. Lee brought it into the living-room and opened it. It contained the original script of "Sin," and all Venner's letters to Siebert Ackroyd.

"How did you get them?" demanded Cynthia, opening her eyes to their widest.

"A little act of burglary," said Lee blandly. "I have arranged for photostat copies to be made, and they will be back in the Ackroyd files before morning."

Cynthia regarded the untidy script with somber eyes.

Lee handed it first to Fanny, who was an expert in typing. She studied it word by word under a magnifying glass, while Lee with another glass spread the dozen letters on the table.

"These letters appear to have been signed by a man writing with his left hand. All the signatures show the same characteristics, but the letters are better formed towards the last. He has been practicing writing with his left hand."

"As to the letters," said Lee, "they are all brief and they are expressed in a rather dictatorial or peremptory style. He issues his orders as if his agent were a servant." Lee looked at Cynthia affectionately. "A man would hardly take that tone if he were writing to *himself*."

Cynthia refused to be impressed. "If he was clever enough to have thought of the rest, he could assume that, too."

Fanny said: "He used a Royal typewriter of an old model. The type is badly worn, the alignment of letters has become uneven through neglect, and the rubber platen so hardened with age that the period made a hole in the paper every time it was struck."

"Good work!" said Lee.

After further study of the script, Fanny went on: "The person who wrote this was accustomed to typing. He wrote rapidly, but he keeps making the same mistakes all through. It looks as if he had been accustomed to a different keyboard, but that can hardly be, since all makes of typewriters adopted a standardized keyboard some years ago. I can't explain it."

"I can't see the great Mack Townley typing rapidly," said Cynthia.

"Here's a funny thing!" exclaimed Fanny. "Though the type generally is so worn, there is one character that is clear and sharp. It's the exclamation point." She shoved the script over for Lee to see.

"Fine!" said Lee. "That is something definite to go on. The exclamation point is not included in the standard keyboard. The man who used the old typewriter had it put in place of some character he didn't use. He required exclamation points on every page of his play, you see. He would naturally go to one of the Royal service shops to have this done. Such a request cannot be a common one. Perhaps we can trace the old typewriter through this means."

CHAPTER TWENTY-TWO

REPORTS OF A. W.

("This is a new man I have got," remarked Lee to Cynthia. "An actor temporarily out of a job. He's good.")

December 30th.—As soon as I received word from you that Mrs. Mack Townley had applied to the — Agency for an English butler, I went to the agency to register.

I was sent first to a Mrs. Frelinghuysen on Fifth Avenue, and I had considerable difficulty in getting away, because she wanted to engage me. I said I was addicted to snuff, and she let me go. This interview gave me more assurance in facing Mrs. Townley, to whom I was next sent. Mrs. T. is a very beautiful woman but she is not a lady born, and she has an arrogant and disagreeable manner towards servants. However, that was nothing to me. I made the right answers and was instructed to come to work yesterday afternoon.

On my arrival at the apartment I was turned over to the other servants. There was a lot of gossip among them about the play "Sin," but of course they don't know anything—except, perhaps, Antoinette, who accompanies her mistress to the theater every night. Antoinette said very mysteriously that

Townley knows who really wrote the play, and so does Mrs. T., and that she is holding the knowledge over his head. However, they expect to make a quarter of a million out of it, and neither is going to say or do anything which will jeopardize that.

Shortly after eight o'clock Mr. and Mrs. departed for the theater taking Antoinette with them, and I saw no more of them last night. Mrs. T. sent Antoinette home after the performance and she herself didn't come in until near four. Her husband was waiting for her, and there was a scene. There were no witnesses to it so I cannot give you any details.

December 31st (Sunday).—Neither of them showed themselves yesterday until lunch. They appeared to be reconciled.

After lunch they both went out. Mrs. Townley had to go to the theater for the matinee, and Townley told her he was meeting Siebert Ackroyd at the Conradi-Windermere for the purpose of signing the movie contracts with the Paramount officials.

At dinner last night the following conversation took place between them. I don't understand it, but pass it along for what it may be worth. Townley said: "I am considering a play by Jules Taschereau as a vehicle for you later on." She said: "Hadn't you better let me read it before you make up your mind?" He said: "Surely! It isn't a good play, but it will make money. The woman's part is the whole thing. Your part in 'Sin' isn't worthy of you. Now that you have created it, you could retire and do this other thing." Mrs. Townley, leaning her chin on her palm, said with a dreamy air: "Of course it's not much of a part, but I love it! I hear his dear voice in every line!" Townley flew into a passion and pounded the table. "—! Am I to have him thrown in my face forever!"

She looked at him contemptuously and said: "Are you jealous of the dead?" Then she saw me and dismissed me from the room.

A. W.

When Cynthia read this report her ideas underwent a violent process of readjustment. "Mack Townley?" she muttered. Then in a different tone: "*Mack Townley! It was he!*"

Lee shrugged deprecatingly.

"But it is clear from this that both Mack Townley and his wife know that 'Sin' is my father's play."

"Surely. However, that doesn't prove that Mack killed him. You must remember that Gavin and Mack were associated for nearly twenty years in putting on plays. It is possible that when this play was offered to Mack he recognized it as Gavin's work from internal evidence, just as you did."

"And never denounced the murderer and thief!"

"My dear," said Lee, "Mack's trained eye would tell him at a glance that there was a fortune in the play, whoever wrote it."

"Ah, human nature is disgusting!" exclaimed Cynthia in her bitterness.

"Oh, not always!" protested Lee.

CHAPTER TWENTY-THREE

B<small>RIEFER REPORTS.</small>

From Detective-Sergeant J.

It's a cinch to watch George Hillman because his life
is so regular. The danger of this job is, it's too easy;
I find myself falling asleep over it. Since he returned
to town he has been sticking closely to business at
the Harvest Restaurant. A couple of weeks ago they
decided to keep it open all night, as there is no other
all-night eating-place in the neighborhood. The
move has been very profitable. I should estimate that
they were grossing well over two thousand a week
now. Hillman don't seem to take any pleasure in
their prosperity. He's as worried-looking as ever.

Yesterday he departed from his routine. Coming
out of his house about six o'clock he proceeded to
the East Side subway and took a down-town express.
At Eighty-sixth he changed to local and got out at
Fifty-first Street. I followed him to the Conradi-
Windermere Hotel and was just behind him when
he asked at the desk for Miss Gail Garrett. The clerk
told him that Miss Garrett no longer lived there, and
that they didn't have her present address. He re-
ferred Hillman to Mr. Bittner, her manager. Hillman
then entered a telephone booth. The adjoining

booths were full and I was unable to overhear the conversation, but I assumed that he was calling Bittner's apartment. He then took a Lexington Avenue bus to Twenty-fifth Street and entered an old hotel called the Engstrom, a crummy joint, badly run down. I was just behind him. He asked for Miss Garrett and after telephoning upstairs, they told him she was out. But I could tell (and so could he) that the telephone girl had had her on the wire.

I made some fake inquiry of the clerk and followed Hillman out of the hotel. He looked sunk. For over an hour he wandered aimlessly along the streets of that neighborhood; Lexington Avenue, Twenty-eighth Street, Fifth Avenue, Twenty-third, and so on. At ten past eight he returned to the Engstrom. I couldn't follow him in a second time because the clerk would certainly have got on to me. Anyhow, he was turned away a second time and came out looking depressed. It was now time to go to work, and he took the subway back to the Bronx.

From M. O'B.

I went to the office of the — Co., publishers, to fish for a little information. The man who received me said they were no longer publishers for Emmett Gundy. "Oh, has he left you?" I said. "Hardly that," the man said with a sour smile. "His last novel was not profitable and we didn't care to go on with him. You had better go to Miss Flora Chisholm, his agent, for further information." Miss Chisholm's office is on the seventh floor of the New York Central Building. Here I made out to be the representative of a new publishing house. I asked her if she had placed Mr. Gundy's last novel. No, she had not, but several publishers were interested in it. She gave me a sales talk, and offered to send the script to my office. "You can have this fine novel on very easy terms," she said. I told her not to send it until I let her know.

It appears Gundy is hard up, but not entirely without money. Acts like a man whose time hangs heavy on his hands. About noon I see him come to his window in his pajamas, yawning and stretching. When he comes out of the house he always looks the pink of perfection. On the night of the 28th he attended a party given by the Mack Townleys at the Andorra. He spends a lot of time in the cheap movie houses on West Forty-second Street. On the 30th he spent the entire afternoon and evening going from one house to another. On the morning of the 27th I trailed him to the office of his agent, Miss Chisholm, in the New York Central Building. I couldn't wait in the upstairs corridor for him to come out because it was empty. So I stood in the main lobby downstairs watching the elevators. All the elevators serving the seventh floor come down in the same alcove, and I didn't see how he could get by me. But he never came down. After waiting a couple of hours I put in a fake call to Miss Chisholm's office. She said he had been there but had left immediately. On the 29th the same thing happened again. This was the afternoon. He went to his agent's office and never came down again. I waited until I saw Miss Chisholm and her stenographer going home and I knew the office was closed.

M. O'B.

"This man is a fool," remarked Lee. "It has not occurred to him that if Emmett discovered he was being trailed all he had to do was to walk upstairs and take an elevator that would land him in a different part of the lobby. I must find a better man."

From V. P.

. . . . .

Alan Talbert has a front of brass. In spite of everything that has been published in the newspapers, he
is still going around asserting with a smooth face
that he wrote "Sin," and no amount of razzing can
break him down. He can find plenty who pretend to
believe him; to a certain class of people he's a hero
because he has had so much publicity. He has no
difficulty in finding some rich woman (not too
young) to take him on a round of the most expensive hot spots every night.

. . . . .

Amongst all this chatter I heard Alan say one thing
that may or may not be of interest to you. It was at
the bar of the Colony Restaurant. An overstuffed
dame upholstered in sables was feeding Alan there
and they had lined up for a quick one before going
in. Next to Alan stood Rufus Cooley, the critic, who
said, laughing:

"You will never make me believe that you wrote
it! 'Sin' was turned out by a more finished hand than
yours, my boy!"

"That is Gavin Dordress' influence," said Alan.
"You forget that I worked under Gavin for years. He
used to call me his successor. He helped me a lot
with this play. The quiet effectiveness of the big
scenes that you have all spoken of is due to Gavin. I
owe Gavin everything."

Rufus actually seemed to be impressed by this.
"Gavin Dordress!" he said, stroking his chin. "I never
thought of that! . . . Dordress? Why, of course! of
course!"

V. P.

CHAPTER TWENTY-FOUR

Report of E. B. H.

December 31st.—I didn't report earlier because I was unable to establish contact with my man. Siebert Ackroyd lives at the Madison along with many another well-to-do young man about town. I thought my best line would be that of the rich young idler and I went to the Madison on Friday morning and took a suite. Ackroyd has lived there for several years and is well known to the staff. The servants talk about him because he has been so much in the news lately. They say that a change has come over him. One of the most popular young fellows in that set, he has turned solitary and morose. In view of the great success of his play "Sin" nobody can understand it. They say that he stood to pull down a commission of ten grand from the movie rights alone. They say he is drinking too much, and they resent it because he doesn't do his drinking at the Madison.

After dinner on Friday night he started out from his hotel on foot, and I after him. He led me to a saloon on Third Avenue. He stood down at the end of the bar away from everybody and ordered a straight rye. I could see by the ugly look in his eyes that it would be foolish to speak to him. He remained there a couple of hours ordering one whisky after another without any visible effect, and saying nothing. He then went home and presumably to bed.

On Saturday evening he didn't show up at the hotel for dinner. I looked in at the Third Avenue saloon just on the chance, and there he was in the same place, scowling at his drink. So I ordered one and stood there scowling at mine, likewise, making out not to notice him at all. This night I was in luck because there was three young roughs in the place who were pretty tight. They passed some remarks about Ackroyd because they didn't like his high-toned style, but he didn't hear them. Afterwards the three were scuffling in the back of the room and one of them bumped against Ackroyd. He was just drunk enough and sore enough to turn and cuss the fellow out, and all three of them were ready to mix it up with him then.

That was my chance. I lined up alongside Ackroyd saying I would see fair play, and between us we stretched all three of them. We and the bartender then threw them into the street. "Let's go over to the Madison," he said. "I live there." "So do I," I said. "We won't go into the Madison bar," he said, "I know too many of those guys. I'm fed up with them. We'll go up in my room and order a bottle."

That suited me all right. But even up in his room with a bottle of Canadian Club between us, he had little to say. He apologized for being such poor company, and I said: "That's all right with me. I don't feel like talking, myself." That caught his attention and he said: "So you're feeling low, too, eh? What is it? Woman trouble?" I nodded, and he thrust out his hand. "Put it there, fellow!" He filled up my glass and his own. "After all, whisky's a fellow's best friend," he said.

From that he went on to tell me a little about a girl of his, but only in general terms, no particulars. "I had a girl," he said, "and I went all out for her. God! how I loved her! I was prepared to lie, to steal, to kill for that woman, and she, oh, she was the perfect lady throughout. All this money that's rolling in on me I aimed to spend on her. It's only a mockery now."

"Maybe she might change her mind now," I suggested. "No, she has plenty of her own," he said. "She isn't mercenary. Only too goddamned ladylike! She turned me down because I was too wicked and violent for her taste. She wants a tame man." "Did she have any special reason?" I asked. "Oh, I've done things I wouldn't want her to know about," he said, "but she could have made anything she wanted of me! The hell with her! She had ice in her veins!"

When she had read this far, Cynthia broke down in stormy weeping. "This is intolerable!" she cried. "It's so wicked and untrue! I hate him for it! I hate him!"

Lee reached for the report. "Why read any further?"

Cynthia clung to it. "I want to know the worst about him." She read on:

"There was always trouble between this girl and me," Ackroyd continued. "I loved her too goddamned much, that was the reason. She couldn't understand it. She didn't know that if she had given me love it would have softened me like a magic charm. There was a certain obstacle in the way that drove me savage." "What kind of obstacle?" I asked. "Never mind," he said. "It was there. Then it was unexpectedly removed and I thought everything would be all right between us. But no! She backed and she filled; she blew hot and cold. Finally she

made up her mind that I was a crook and that was
the end."

"Were you a crook?" I asked with a grin.

"Sure," he said. "Aren't we all?" "What particular
kind of crookedness was it that she jibbed at?" I
asked. The innocent-sounding question aroused his
suspicions. "Oh, everything," he said, and shut up
like a clam. For a while I talked about other things
to smooth him down, and then I beat it.

E. B. H.

"This is worse than I had expected," murmured Cynthia. "There
is a phrase here: 'I aimed to spend this money on her.' That proves
that Siebert had been planning the crime for weeks."

"It is possible," said Lee.

"You were right about Mack Townley," she went on. "He didn't
do it. What Siebert said to this man is as good as a confession."

"I have expressed no opinion either one way or the other," said
Lee. "Let us keep open minds."

CHAPTER TWENTY-FIVE

Report of R. F. S.

The Royal Typewriter Company has two service shops in New York. I visited both of them without result. No employee could remember having received an order to add an exclamation point to the keyboard of an old Royal machine. Other Royal shops in the New York district are in Brooklyn and Newark, N. J. In Newark I finally struck pay dirt. The machinist in charge of repairs remembered the man who wanted an exclamation point, though it was about two months ago, he said, when this customer came in. It was fixed in the machinist's mind because the order was an unusual one, and because the customer was such a queer-looking guy.

His description of the man tallies with other descriptions of the man in the yellow overcoat. The machinist said he brought the typewriter in under his arm, and carried it out again when it was fixed. It was in bad order and the machinist tried to get an order to repair it, or to sell the customer a better machine. But he had no money, he said; all he wanted was an exclamation point, "because he had to write dialogue."

The customer's actions were so mysterious the machinist thought maybe the typewriter was stolen, and he checked it with the list of stolen machines that is furnished to all branch offices. But the number wasn't on the list. The serial number of the machine was 117284. It was of the model that was put out in 1922 and had had hard usage. Scratched in the paint on the under side of the frame were the words "Reliable O. S. Co."

The New York telephone directory furnished the name of a Reliable Office Supply Company on Sixth Avenue and I went up there on the chance. I was in luck. This is the store where the man in the yellow overcoat bought the typewriter; the date was November 8th. ["Two days after Gavin was killed," remarked Lee.] The store, which is near the corner of Forty-ninth Street, sells all makes of second-hand type writers. The salesman remembered this customer because of his queer appearance. A few minutes after he left he returned and bought a box of typewriter paper and a dozen sheets of carbon. This suggests that he had established himself somewhere near by.

I made inquiries in Forty-ninth Street, I got no line on his hangout, if any, but I found where he had left an old pair of shoes to be patched at a repair shop in that street. This was a week ago. I ought to have assistance in watching the shop in case he comes for the shoes.

R. F. S.

CHAPTER TWENTY-SIX

AT THE HOSPITAL Cynthia served as aide to the doctors of the neurological clinic. Her job was to receive the out-patients, to enter their names, to arrange for their appointments with the doctors, and to keep their case histories. Hundreds of cases passed through her hands weekly, but they were still individual to her and human.

Mrs. Rohan and her son Patsy were among the regular attendants at the clinic. They had been coming once a week for a long time past. Both had epilepsy. The mother, a widow, had the appearance of a normal woman, but was crushed with misfortune and overwork; the boy was one of Cynthia's most repellent cases. Subnormal mentally and physically, he was seventeen years old, but except for the sprouting mustache on his lip looked like a boy of twelve. There was a furtive glitter in his eye, but he scarcely ever spoke. At home there were other children whom Cynthia had never seen. None of these children should have been born; but there they were, and it was not their fault.

On Monday afternoon near closing time Patsy turned up at the clinic alone. The Rohans had no appointment that day. He hung about, peeping around the corner of the corridor until Cynthia caught sight of him and beckoned him to her desk. He slunk forward with his upper lip lifted like a frightened animal's.

"Mom's sick," he blurted out.

Cynthia drew a long breath in the effort to conquer her repulsion. "What's the matter with her?" she asked.

"I dunno. She's on the bed. She can't get up. The kids is crying because they ain't eaten since morning."

Cynthia glanced at her watch. "All right. You run home and tell your mother I'll be there in a quarter of an hour. I'll give you money to buy milk and crackers for the children to keep them quiet until I come."

Patsy cringed. "I better take you there," he said. "It's a hard place to find."

"All right," said Cynthia. "Sit down until I'm ready."

They left the hospital together. In the street Cynthia hailed a taxi and Patsy grinned.

"I never rode in one of them before."

He gave an address in the northeast corner of the island which Cynthia knew to be one of the most depressed areas in the city. After they had started he said uneasily:

"Tell the guy to stop at the corner of First Avenue. If we was to stop in front of my house the street kids would razz the life out of me."

Cynthia passed the word to the driver. She kept to her corner of the cab. The boy was clean enough—his hard-working mother saw to that, but he seemed to emanate a moral decay. Meanwhile he was enjoying the drive.

They got out on First Avenue and headed east. Cynthia had never visited this particular block. The tenement houses were ancient and decaying; some of them, condemned by the authorities, had their doors and windows boarded up; occasionally a house had been pulled down, leaving a gap in the row like a missing tooth. It had grown dark. The night was unseasonably mild; doors and windows stood open; children were playing in the street. Patsy, glancing at the big boys in terror, pressed against Cynthia. She took his hand, though his touch made her flesh crawl. Coming to a small grocery store, she said:

"I'll get milk and crackers here for the children."

"Don't stop! Don't stop!" he said with an odd excitement. "After I take you to my mom I'll come back and get it."

They went on.

He led her into an old house whose greasy doorway was flush with the sidewalk. Inside, a dim bulb lighted a long, narrow hall with a splintery floor. A steep stairway went up at the side. Cynthia made for the stairway, but the boy pulled her past it. "It's in the back," he said. "We live in a back-yard tenement."

The light of the single bulb scarcely penetrated to the back of the hall. Suddenly Cynthia realized that something was wrong, and stopped. She could see through an open door at the back of the hall. There was no house in the rear, but only a littered yard, a broken fence, and the rear of a boarded-up house fronting on the next street.

"You have been lying to me . . . !" she began.

She got no further. There was a figure lurking under the stairs. A heavy blow descended on her head, stunning her. She did not lose consciousness altogether, but all her faculties were paralyzed except that of hearing. The cellar door beside her was thrown back and she was hastily dragged down the stairs. She could hear her own heels thudding from step to step. The boy pulled the door shut and ran down after her.

In the cellar she was flung on her face on the earthen floor and the man knelt on her back, crushing the breath out of her. He drew a cloth of some sort over her mouth. Her senses were returning to her. As she opened her mouth to scream, he jerked the cloth between her teeth, almost splitting her lips and choking off all sounds. He pulled her hands behind her to tie them.

"Light the candle," he growled.

A match was struck and a little light spread around. The boy placed the stub of a candle on the earth. His subhuman face was wreathed in a grin. Cynthia could not see the man who was holding her down. He said in his husky whisper:

"Set the yard door open."

The boy went away. The man was swiftly tying Cynthia's wrists and ankles together. When the boy returned the man said:

"Watch the cellar stairs."

"Nobody comes down here but the gas man," said the boy.

"Never mind. Watch the stairs."

"Where's my money?" asked the boy.

"Open her pocketbook."

After a moment the boy said: "There's only twenty-three dollars in it."

"All right, take it and get."

"You promised me a hundred," whined the boy.

"Get out!" growled the man.

The boy began to cry. "If you don't give me my hundred I'll tell!" he wailed.

The man sprang to his feet with a muttered oath. The boy started to run, but was overtaken in two strides. They had passed out of Cynthia's range of vision, but she heard the sickly crack of something hard on a human skull, and the soft collapse of a body on the earth.

The man returned to her. When he finished his knots he turned her over on her back and then for the first, as he bent over her, Cynthia saw him; the tall hulking frame in the shapeless yellow coat, the queer cap pulled close over his head. He had a black handkerchief tied over the lower part of his face; his glasses glittered in the candle-light, hiding the expression of his eyes. Instinctively Cynthia screamed with all her might, but only a strangled groan issued through the gag. The man pulled a gun from his pocket, and showed it to her lying on his palm.

"Keep quiet," he whispered hoarsely, "or you'll get what the boy got."

Looking beyond her feet, she saw the pitiful thin figure sprawling on the foul earth. Blood was running through his sparse hair. She became quiet. She could not make noise enough to be heard; she wanted to save her strength.

Stepping over her body, the man trod out the candle flame. Returning, he took her under the arms and dragged her to a stone stair at the back of the cellar. He dropped her here and went ahead to investigate. Returning, he dragged her out into the open yard. As the back wall of the tenement rose before her with lights in a score of kitchen windows, Cynthia struggled with all her force and endeavored to scream again. The man struck her savagely and she became quiet. It was useless.

He dragged her across to the broken fence, and lifting her up coolly dropped her on the other side. Though he was such a big fellow, he was panting from his exertions. This was the yard of the abandoned house. It was heaped with piles of rubbish over which the man dragged her anyhow. They came to another cellar door. He pulled her through it and down a half stair, and letting her fall on a cement floor, went back to shut the door. It had glass panes, and the upper part of his body was silhouetted against it. He lingered there, apparently stuffing the cracks of the door to prevent any sounds from escaping.

At this moment Cynthia's heart was ready to break with despair. Bound and gagged in the cellar of an abandoned house; at the mercy of an armed madman. Then she discovered that in her rough passage across the yard the ropes around her ankles had loosened, and hope stirred in her again. While the man was working at the door, she drew her legs up behind her, and hooking fingers under a strand of the rope, managed to work it over a heel. The rest was easy. When he came down the cellar steps her legs were free.

He struck a match in order to find her. In the brief flash of light Cynthia saw a dozen paces away, an open stairway leading up. She scrambled to her feet and raced for it. The man came after her, cursing, but his match went out and he couldn't stop to light another. He sprawled over the bottom steps. Drawing his gun, he fired in the direction of Cynthia's racing feet, but the shot went wild. Cynthia gained the ground floor hall of the house and leaned against the wall, trembling. The crash of the shot seemed to turn her blood to water.

Presently she heard him softly inching up the cellar stairs. Feeling her way along the hall with her forehead, she came to an open door and slipped through it. She discovered that all the doors and windows sashes had been taken out and stacked against the walls. At the top of the stairs the man struck a match, but remained standing and listening, uncertain which way Cynthia had gone.

The rope around Cynthia's wrists was partly loosened. Backing up to one of the doors leaning against the wail, she hooked a strand of the rope over the door handle and brought down her hands with a sharp jerk. The pull almost dislocated her wrists, but the rope came off and her hands were free. The man heard the sound, and started towards the door of the room she was in, striking a match. Feeling her way around the wall, she found another door and passed through it.

The man was following her and the dreadful thought came to her that he had her trapped in a room with only one door. But there was another room beyond it, and a fourth room beyond that. This was a front room; thin cracks of light showed between the planks nailed in the window openings, and sounds of the street came through, filling Cynthia with a sickness of longing. She had loosened the gag until it fell around her neck but she uttered no cry. Long before help could reach her from the outside, the man with the gun would have been upon her.

This front room had a door opening on the main corridor of the house, and she stood there listening. For some moments she had heard no sound of creeping feet or striking matches, and she didn't know where the man was. Listening somewhere, like herself. Cynthia's desperately sharpened wits had figured out the ground plan of this house. She knew that the cellar stairs were to the rear of the corridor and about forty feet from where she stood. She had seen the man stuffing the cracks of the door into the yard below, but she had not heard him lock that door. Apparently he had no key to it. If she could reach it first, safety lay on the other side. It was worth trying. She slipped off her shoes.

Nerving herself up to it, she dashed for the head of the stairs. The man, waiting somewhere in the rear, heard her and divined her intention. He was nearer the stairs; they collided at the top and he flung an arm around her. His panting breath was in her face. She sensed that his gun was in his other hand. He was between her and the stairs. Cynthia, with the strength of desperation, launched her body against his at the same time gripping the door frame. He toppled, clutching at her wildly. His hold was torn loose and he went over backwards. His gun discharged as he fell.

An absolute silence succeeded the crash. Cynthia, backing out of line of possible further shots, prayed that he might be seriously injured. Moments passed and she could hear nothing. Unable to bear the suspense, she moved one of the doors to the head of the stairs and let it slide down on its edge. It slapped over on the concrete below. So he was not on the stairs. Cynthia went down a few steps and looked towards the rear of the cellar. At the same moment the man struck a match to see what had caused the clatter on the stairs. He was lying in wait for her at the yard door, the only way out.

Drawing back out of sight, Cynthia softly returned to the front room on the first floor. Picking up another door, she launched it on edge like a battering ram against one of the planks over the window. The plank creaked but held fast. Before she could strike a second blow she heard him running up the cellar stairs. Dropping the door, she softly retreated through the rooms into the rear. He ran straight through the corridor into the front room, and joy welled up in her heart. The way out was clear!

She ran down the stairs on stockinged feet, and across the cellar. He had wedged a stick under the handle of the door to hold it fast, but it was the work of a second to kick that aside, and she breathed the sweet outer air again. She heard him plunging down the stairs, and scrambled anyhow over the piles of rubbish in the yard; fell over the fence, found the doorway to the house in front, and running through it, gained the sidewalk. There were people standing about. She sank down, fainting.

CHAPTER TWENTY-SEVEN

WHEN CYNTHIA OPENED HER EYES AGAIN it was to find the blessed Irish face of a policeman bending over her. The people of the neighborhood were staring down at her curiously. "What happened, Miss?" asked the policeman.

"A man seized me," she stammered. "He dragged me into an abandoned house in the next street. He killed Patsy Rohan."

A murmur of horror traveled around the circle. "What man?" asked the policeman.

"A big man. Wore a yellow overcoat, cap pulled down close over his head."

Several voices spoke up at once: "I saw him! He come out of the house and went down towards the river."

A radio car with two more policemen had drawn up at the curb alongside. Word was passed to the driver and they set off to look for the man.

Cynthia's policeman asked: "Where do you live, Miss?"

Afraid of entering her own place alone, she gave the address of Lee's apartment.

"Amos Lee Mappin!" said the policeman, surprised. "I read about him. I'll take you there."

A taxi was brought from First Avenue and they got in.

Lee lived on an upper floor of one of the lofty apartment houses overlooking the East River. When they arrived at the door, he paled at the sight of Cynthia's limp figure, and the arms that took her trembled. He laid her on a couch in his living-room. The police-man told his story.

Lee asked a few pointed questions; made no comment. "Miss Dordress will be available for questioning any time she may be needed," he told the policeman.

When he had gone, Lee telephoned to Headquarters. He was told that Inspector Loasby had gone to the station house of the twenty-fifth precinct to direct the search for the murderer. Lee got him there, and Loasby told him that the man in the yellow over-coat had not been apprehended. He had last been seen getting in a taxi which headed south on East River Drive. A general alarm had been sent out for him.

"That's not likely to produce anything," said Lee. "He was dis-guised, of course. He will change it now."

Loasby went on to say that the body of Patsy Rohan had been found in the cellar. The boy's mother, who lived upstairs, was dazed by what had happened. No suspicion attached to her in the minds of the police.

"I'll pay for the wretch's burial," said Lee. "Don't mention my name."

When the police had searched the abandoned house in the next street, Loasby said, they found on the cement floor at the foot of the cellar stairs, a small flat key with a number cut in the shaft, number 415.

"A hotel key?" asked Lee.

"No. Hotel keys have the name of the hotel engraved on them. This key is too small and thin for a room key."

"I'll come up and take a look at it," said Lee.

Returning to Cynthia, he said: "The man has not been caught. Evidently he worked single-handed. Watching the clinic for days past, I take it. In the imbecile boy he found just the tool he needed."

"Why did he attack me?" murmured Cynthia.

"He was afraid. We are getting too close to him. He doesn't know that I have consulted the police. He thought if he could make away with you, then with me, he would be safe. And, O God! how

nearly he succeeded with you! We might never have found you!"
He struggled with his feelings.

"Did you have a small key marked four hundred and fifteen?"
he asked in his customary matter-of-fact voice.

"No," she said. "Only my apartment key. That was in the bag
they took."

"The brute will be desperate now," said Lee. "We must act
quickly. I'll send for Fanny to stay with you. Jermyn will take care
of you both. You are quite safe here."

"You are going out?" she said, freshly terrified.

"Only to see Loasby."

"Oh, Lee, be careful! If anything happened to you. . . !"

"Don't worry!" he said grimly. "If he tries it with me I'll be ready
for him."

Telling his man Jermyn to phone Miss Parran to come and stay
with Cynthia, and not to let anybody else into the apartment until
he returned, Lee taxied up to Harlem.

Loasby was in the captain's private office, attended by Riordan,
a young detective who acted as his secretary and aide. Both were
in plain clothes. The handsome Inspector was angered by this dirty
crime and inclined to blame Lee for having permitted it. Lee ignored his ill-humor. As soon as Lee laid eyes on the key found by
the police, he said: "I know what sort of key that is. I have often
used them. They are for the lock boxes in railway stations where
you drop a dime and check your bag."

"They have such boxes in fifty places around town," said Loasby,
scowling.

"They are all put out by the same company. Phone quick to the
main office and ask where box number four hundred and fifteen
is. Arrange to have a watch put on it."

Riordan did the telephoning. "Pennsylvania Terminal," he reported.

"Come on!" said Lee, making for the door.

Loasby and Riordan followed. "If he's lost the key," Loasby
grumbled, "he won't go back to the box."

"Man," said Lee, "with a general alarm out for him, if his other clothes are in that box it's a matter of life and death for him to get them."

In a red police car with blue searchlight and screaming siren they made the Pennsylvania Terminal in nine minutes. In the local office of the checking company they were faced by a frightened manager.

"You're too late," he stammered. "He's been and got his things. I'm sorry. I . . . I didn't know he was wanted."

Lee clenched his teeth together and silently cursed their luck.

"What sort of man?" demanded the Inspector.

The manager repeated the too-familiar description of the man in the yellow overcoat. "He said he had lost his key," he went on. "He was in a hurry to catch a train. He described everything that was in the box and offered to pay for a new lock. So I opened the box for him. That is our rule."

"What was in it?" asked Lee.

"A yellow gladstone bag, sir, considerably scuffed and worn. It contained a black vicuña overcoat, a black soft hat rolled up, a blue cheviot suit, black shoes and socks, a white shirt that had already been worn, with collar attached, a blue tie, a tin box . . ."

"What was in the box?"

"I didn't open it."

"How long ago was this?"

"Less than half an hour, sir."

"Didn't it strike you as strange," said the Inspector sternly, "that a man looking like that should have such fine clothes?"

"I thought they were his Sunday clothes, sir."

"You should. . . ."

Lee shut the Inspector off. "I know why he chose the Pennsylvania station to check his things. Downstairs they have rooms for the convenience of travelers who wish to change their clothes. He may still be there. Come on!"

Lee, Loasby, and Riordan hastened to the stairway on the north side of the concourse and ran down. The spotless glass-tiled lavatory

opened off the basement corridor. It was lined down to the far end
with a row of little dressing-rooms, each having a mahogany door
with a slot machine in the lock to receive dimes. Halfway down the
long row there was an arched opening leading to another division
of the lavatory. The attendant of the place was standing near the
entrance. Loasby gave him a brief flash of the gold badge.

"Have you seen a man in here during the last half hour wearing
a yellowish kind of overcoat?" he asked in a low voice.

The man shook his head. "I got to watch the nickel side, too,
Inspector, I don't see them all."

"This was an unusual-looking man; a hulking fellow, stoop-
shouldered; wore a leather helmet pulled down close over his head,
thick spectacles, was carrying an old Gladstone bag."

"Yeah, I seen such a one," said the man suddenly. "Here on the
dime side. He went into a box halfway down. It would be number
nine or ten or eleven. For all I know he's still there."

Before the attendant finished speaking, a door in the middle of
the long row silently opened, and like a shadow, a tall man slipped
swiftly across the narrow space and through the opening into the
other side of the lavatory. He had his head turned from them, and
they could not see his face. Black hat, black overcoat; Lee's suspicions were aroused. "Look in that room!" he shouted.

The Inspector and Riordan dashed toward the door of the box.
"Stop that man!" they cried. Lee, figuring that he would have to
come out into the corridor through the next opening, turned in the
other direction to head him off.

He collided with the running man in the next opening to the
corridor. The man was holding an arm over his face. He charged
full tilt into Lee, sending him sprawling on his back in the corridor, while he sprang for the stairs. When Lee got his breath the
man was disappearing around the top of the stairs. Lee added his
voice to the bellowing Inspector, "Stop that man!" A whole row of
bootblacks stopped work and leaped up the stairs, brushes and rags
in hand. The customers climbed out of the chairs and followed. Up
above the cry was taken up: "Stop that man!"

The Inspector and Riordan appeared out of the lavatory. "All his stuff was in the box," Loasby muttered. When they reached the great concourse above, he had another glimpse of the man as he headed obliquely across for the doors leading to the outer concourse. He was slimmer than Lee expected, and not stoop-shouldered at all. Desperation was lending him the speed of a deer. A door obediently opened for him and he disappeared through it. The cries were echoing from end to end of the vast hall; "Stop that man!" Men came running from every direction to join the chase. The crowd got tangled up in the mechanical doors and the fugitive gained on them.

When Lee reached the outer concourse, the man had almost got to the Thirty-first Street side of the building. Men directly in his path scuttled out of the way, and fell in at a safe distance behind him. The crowd was roaring. The fugitive was clever enough not to spring up the wide stairs to the street, where he would certainly have been caught. Running under the stairway, he plunged down the steps leading to the mezzanine corridor that bisects the huge building from side to side. This is the busiest part of the Terminal, with crowds pouring up from the train platforms below, another crowd waiting to meet friends and more hundreds passing to and from the subway and the taxi landings.

Running alongside Lee, the face of the dignified Inspector had become purple. "If you catch him it means promotion," he shouted to Riordan, and put out a hand to stop Lee. "Let the young men run," he panted. "This is no work for us!"

"I'm not done yet," said Lee. He ran on, leaving Loasby.

Midway through the corridor, there was a side corridor leading in the direction of the subway station a block away. The fugitive had passed out of hearing and the pursuers halted irresolutely. Some said he had headed for the subway, others said straight ahead. The main body decided for the subway and started charging through the tiled corridor. If he had gone that way, they would catch him on the platform, Lee thought, and he, Riordan and a few others kept on towards the Thirty-third Street side where the taxis waited. This part of the mezzanine was less crowded at the moment.

While they were still fifty yards away, through the glass of the doors leading to the taxi platform they saw their man getting into a cab. "Stop that man!" they yelled, but the taxi-driver either could not or did not want to hear, and the cab whirled out of sight into the ramp leading to the street. They piled into the next cab. They found the first cab stopped at the head of the ramp by a red light. Coming up behind it, they leaped out, each with a gun in hand. But the cab ahead was empty. "The so-and-so jumped out and run down Eighth Avenue," said the driver, disgustedly. "I couldn't leave my cab."

In the crowded sidewalk of Eighth Avenue there was no sign of their man. "He has diddled us," growled Lee.

CHAPTER TWENTY-EIGHT

LOASBY PREPARED TO RETURN to Headquarters. "I'd be glad to have you with me," he said to Lee. "I'm organizing a search that will comb this town with fine teeth. Two heads are better than one."

"All right," said Lee. "Let me telephone home first."

Jermyn told him over the wire that Miss Cynthia was all right. Miss Fanny was with her. He had served their dinner and they had eaten well. Nobody had called at the apartment.

"Any telephone calls?"

"One, sir. About fifteen minutes ago a man called up. He wouldn't give his name. Said his initials were R. F. S. and that you would know him. The voice was unfamiliar to me."

"That's all right," said Lee; "a new man that I have working for me. What did he want?"

"Wanted to get in touch with you, sir. Said he had secured an important piece of evidence that he must put in your hands to-night. I suggested that he come to the apartment, but he said he had a man under observation and he couldn't take the time to come up here. But he said he was close to your office, and if you were going to be there any time this evening, he could run over with it. He said he'd call up the office at intervals to see if you were there."

Lee's glum face lightened a little. An important piece of evidence! This R. F. S. was a first-rate operative. "All right," he said to Jermyn. "I'll go right over there and wait an hour for a call. If he should call you again, tell him I'm there. He'll find the door of the building locked, but there's a bell which rings in the hall. I'll come down and let him in."

To Loasby, Lee said: "I've got to go over to my office for an hour. One of my operatives is coming in. He says he has something. I'll see you later."

"Okay," said Loasby.

Lee took a taxi for his office. He rented a suite in an old brownstone dwelling in the Murray Hill section of Madison Avenue, that had been converted into business offices. Strictly speaking, Lee was only an amateur criminologist, but he paid the rent of this place rather than have queer and unsavory characters come to his apartment. He could afford it. His quarters consisted of a large room across the front of the second floor and two little rooms opening off it.

The building was locked up when he got there. Nobody stayed in it at night. As he let himself into the dark stair-hall the thought flitted across his mind: Maybe I'm foolish to come here alone at night. He thrust it away. Nonsense! I'm safely locked in here. If anybody rings the bell I can look out of the window to make sure it's the man I want to see before I go down. I'm armed, and I have the telephone. What could happen to me? And anyhow the murderer is not going to try on anything else tonight after the scare we gave him in the station!

Lee turned on a desk light in his little private office and lit a cigar. On his desk, where Fanny had left them, lay the newly-arrived proofs and the typescript of his forthcoming book, entitled: *Murder Without Reason*. It included half a dozen fantastic homicide cases that he had dug up. He sat down at his desk and pushed the proofs aside while he waited for his telephone call. He had a more pressing case on his mind now.

He drew on his cigar and allowed the smoke to escape slowly. The events of the day forced him to take a new view of the matter. Up until now he had had it in the back of his mind that the murderer of Gavin Dordress was a hired killer. His recent acts suggested that he was the sole head and front of the affair; a man who worked alone; of all types of criminal the most difficult to run down. He appeared to be rendered desperate by the failure of his schemes. Either that or he was an out-and-out madman. Lee scowled. What could a logical mind do with a madman? A new theory began to form in his mind, but he had no evidence to support it. He glanced wishfully at the telephone. If the operative on the trail of the old typewriter had really turned up something, perhaps they could take the murderer in flank. Why didn't the fellow call up?

Suddenly a cold fear struck into Lee's breast. He had heard no distinct sound, but a sixth sense told him that there was somebody in the front room. "Who's there?" he said sharply. No answer came. Only a silence so intense that it seemed to breathe. He jumped up to go in, but thinking better of it, switched off the lights on his desk. Instantly an unseen hand switched off the lights in the front room, plunging the whole suite in darkness. Lee thrust a hand in his pocket only to remember that he had dropped his gun in his overcoat pocket when he came out into Eighth Avenue. He crouched behind his desk, sweating profusely. Fool! Fool! Fool! he thought.

When his eyes became more accustomed to the darkness, he perceived that there was a little light striking into the front room through the thick glass of the corridor. There was no shade on this door. He had left a light burning in the entrance hall of the house, but there was no light on the landing outside his suite. The light was very faint, but sufficient to reveal anybody who might try to steal into his office from in front. Lee was very sure that the man in front could not see him.

Keeping his eye on the door, his hand stole up to the French telephone on his desk, and silently lifted the instrument. The instant he put the receiver to his ear he realized that the line was dead. There was no response from the operator; the wires had been cut. Lee put the instrument back on his desk. It made a little rap on the wood, and in the front room a man softly chuckled. Lee shivered at the sound.

If the man was lying in wait for him just outside the door, there was a possibility that he could creep around through Fanny's room and take him in the rear. He could retrieve his gun on the way. Breathing with open mouth to make no sound, he started creeping on hands and knees towards the closed door. The ten feet was like a journey of ten miles, an inch at a time, and a pause to listen. Arriving at the door, he had a still more difficult task to open it without giving warning.

It finally swung in silently, and he dropped to hands and knees again. He was familiar with the position of every object in Fanny's little room. The door into the front room was standing open. Just outside it stood the hat tree. When Lee stuck his head into the front room he glimpsed against the faint light coming in from the corridor a shadowy form crouching outside the door of his private office. On the other side of Lee hung his overcoat. He softly felt for the pockets—to find them empty. The man had been before him there. Lee retreated into Fanny's office, trembling violently. It was the man's more than human daring that cut the ground from under his feet. Thus to brave him on Lee's own ground!

He got a grip on himself and started creeping back to his own office, meaning to try to escape through the door into the corridor. Suddenly the top light flared on in his room. The man had been feeling around the edge of the door for the switch. Lee snatched up a book from Fanny's desk and flung it at the light. His aim was true; the lamp exploded, and the little room was plunged in darkness again.

Lee went in there, closing the door after him. None too soon, for the light blazed on in Fanny's room behind him. Lee flung himself on the corridor door, but he was unable to open it. The key had been turned in the ordinary lock, and taken away. At that moment the man in Fanny's room swung a chair and smashed the glass in the door. Lee sprang into the front room and turning about, got the corridor door open and slammed it behind him.

He heard the man coming. He realized in a flash that he could not hope to get down the hall and down the lighted stairs without receiving a bullet in his back, and he turned up the stairs. Rounding the corner, he lay down flat on the steps, holding his breath. The heavy ornamental balustrade kept any light from falling on him. The man came charging out of the front room. He had a hand-kerchief tied around the lower part of his face, and a gun in his hand. As he ran he drew a second gun. He paused at the head of the stairs.

Springing to his feet, Lee made a dash back into the front room. He slammed the door and, turning the key in the ordinary lock, threw it away. He heard the man coming and knew he would only have a second or two. Running obliquely across the room, he flung up the outside window of the four. At the same moment the glass of the corridor door crashed and the man put his hand in to feel for the latch. But he could not open the door; he was still held up for a few seconds.

Lee climbed out on the window sill. The street below was al-most empty. A taxicab sped past, and across the road he had a fleet-ing sense of a couple staring at him, transfixed with astonishment. They couldn't help him. Lee's figure was not well adapted for climb-ing, but under the spur of desperation a man can perform won-ders. Stretching his legs to their widest, he found he could get a foot on the sill of the end window of the next house. Still clinging to his own window frame, he got a grip on the next frame, and drew himself across. The window was closed. Smashing in the glass with his knee, he lowered himself into a dark room.

A door slammed back in the room and lights went on. Lee found himself faced by an indignant man in the doorway with a gun in his hand. "What the hell does this mean?" he demanded.

"Don't shoot!" said Lee. "There's a desperate criminal after me. For God's sake get out of this room and get the door shut!"

His voice carried conviction. The man backed out of the room and allowed Lee to follow him.

"Is there a key in this door?" asked Lee.

"Yes."

"Then for God's sake lock it! . . . Is there any other way out of the room?"

"No."

"Thank God!" Lee leaned against the door and closed his eyes.

"Are you crazy?" demanded the angry householder.

"No," said Lee with a weary grin. "Only a little out of breath."

"What's the explanation of this?"

"I'll tell you . . . but please lead me to a telephone first."

There was a telephone in the back room on the same floor. While Lee was using it, his involuntary host watched him suspiciously, gun in hand. Lee called up Headquarters, and got Loasby on the wire. "This is Lee Mappin," he said. Hearing that name, the householder relaxed somewhat, and lowered his gun.

"The fellow was lying in wait for me in my own office," said Lee.

"Good God!" ejaculated Loasby.

"He nearly got me, but I escaped into the house next door. Next door on the south. It's the residence of Mr. . . . ." He looked at his host.

"Sanderson," said he.

"The residence of Mr. Sanderson," Lee went on to Loasby. "For God's sake, furnish me with a guard, Loasby. And put a guard in the foyer of my apartment house."

"Surely," said Loasby. "I'll have four cars there in a jiffy. We'll surround the building where your offices are."

"Just as you like," said Lee, "but he'll be gone. Mr. Sanderson, I am sure, will allow some of your men to pass through his house so they can reach the rear of the building next door."

Sanderson was all friendliness when Lee hung up. The gun was put away. "I know you by reputation, Mr. Mappin," he said. "What a terrible thing to happen!"

"Yes, quite," said Lee. "It would oblige me very much, Mr. Sanderson, if you were to offer me a drink."

CHAPTER TWENTY-NINE

ALMOST INSTANTANEOUSLY, it seemed, the radio cars one after another drew up silently in front of the house. Detectives came to Mr. Sanderson's door, and Lee handed over the key of the adjoining house. Other men passed through Mr. Sanderson's basement and climbed the back fence so that they could command the rear of the office building next door. A few minutes later Loasby came, and Lee told him in detail what had happened.

"So he thinks he can play with us at his pleasure!" said the angry Inspector. "By God! I'll catch this fellow if it's my last act on earth!"

"Surely!" said Lee.

The search, as Lee had expected, was in vain. The disappointed detectives had presently to report that the man had gone, leaving no trace except the glass he had broken. Apparently he had come out by the front door and coolly walked away up the street before the radio cars arrived. Loasby went back to Headquarters, and Lee returned to his office, guarded now by two plain-clothes men, more conspicuous for brawn than for brains. One was red-faced; one saturnine. Lee was his usual calm self again. Except for the two broken panes no damage had been done. Judging from the condition of the drawers of his desk, Lee judged that the man had gone through his papers; however, everything of importance was locked in the safe.

The two officers effected a temporary splice in the cut telephone wires, and Lee called up his operative, Smither, who signed his reports R. F. S. He found him at home.

"Smither," said Lee, "my servant tells me that a man giving your initials called me up at my apartment this evening, and said that he had discovered an important piece of evidence that he wanted to put in my hands tonight. How about it?"

"Why, Mr. Mappin, it's all a fake!" said the surprised Smither. "I never called you up. As a matter of fact, I haven't had any luck today. Our man never came for the shoes."

"That is what I assumed," said Lee. "You are my principal dependence in this case, Smither. Can you taxi right down to my office to talk things over with me?"

"Surely, Mr. Mappin."

Smither was a small, meager man of fifty with a gloomy expression; no genius, but a dependable fellow. He opened his eyes when he saw the smashed doors.

"Yes, our friend made a raid here tonight," said Lee.

"The man in the yellow overcoat!"

"The very same. We've got the overcoat but we haven't got him."

"What a nerve!" murmured Smither. "Are the police on his trail?"

"They are," said Lee. "But I feel that they will never catch up with him from behind. It's up to you and me to come on him from an unexpected quarter. You haven't located his hangout?"

Smither shook his head.

Lee gave him a cigar and took one himself. "All you found was a pair of old shoes," he said.

"The shoes are out of my hands now," remarked Smither. "Headquarters has men watching the store all the time it is open. They have arranged with the man who runs the store to signal them if anybody presents a ticket for those shoes."

"Right," said Lee. "But he will never call for them now . . . Let me see . . . Forty-ninth Street is the regular route from Broadway over to Radio City and the sidewalk is full all day. Consequently the character of the street has changed very rapidly during the last year or two. Little modern store fronts have been put in all along the way. But above the stores most of the old buildings remain as they were. That block in Forty-ninth Street always was rather miscellaneous. There are some queer lodgings in those old buildings, Smither, and I am sure that is where our man had one of his hangouts."

"One of his hangouts?"

"His yellow-overcoat hangout. The overcoat was part of a disguise, and he only used that room when he was wearing it. Did you examine the shoes?"

"Yes, sir."

"What did you get from them?"

"Nothing that I could use, sir."

"Old shoes are very characteristic."

"Sure they are. But they don't tell you where the wearer's hangout is."

"Ordinarily, no. Still I think it's worth a trip up to Forty-ninth Street. Let's go take another look at those shoes, Smither."

"Okay, Mr. Mappin."

One of the brawny detectives went with them, the red-faced one, the other being left on guard in Lee's office. The three men descended from their taxi at the Sixth Avenue corner and started west through Forty-ninth Street. The shoe-repair shop was not far. It was one of the usual sort, presided over by an Italian padrone.

Smither was known to the Italian in charge of the place, and he brought out the shoes on request. A unique pair of shoes, bright yellow in color, and made on a toothpick-pointed last. "He wore these on his earlier forays," said Lee. "They went well with the rest of the outfit."

"A foreign guy," put in the Italian; "no Americano like us."

While Lee was examining the shoes, the detective on watch outside came in with a questioning air, showing how good a watch he was keeping. He and the other detective established contact, and the first man went out to resume his vigil.

"Almost ready to go to pieces," said Lee, inspecting the shoes. "He picked them up second hand somewhere. Look as if they hadn't been cleaned since. Resoled more than once, and are near ready for another."

"I tella him a need new sole," said the Italian. "Only want little patches, he say. Gotta no mon'."

Lee pursued his examination with the glass. "There are particles of sawdust caught between the welt and the sole; some fresh, some blackened with dirt. Smither, this man walked in sawdust on a number of occasions spread over a considerable period of time. Where would you find sawdust in New York?"

"In a planing and finishing mill."

Lee shook his head. "Take a look through the glass. These are coarse flakes of sawdust, like that chewed out by a big saw when it goes through a log."

"There are no logs sawed up around New York."

"Quite so. But sawdust like this is shipped to the city for a variety of purposes." Lee studied for a while, murmuring to himself: "Sawdust underfoot . . . sawdust underfoot. . . . Smither," he said, raising his head, "sometimes a storekeeper with a nice tile or mosaic floor spreads sawdust in wet weather to protect it from the muddy feet of his customers."

"That's right, sir."

"There's been a lot of rain this fall. Let's see what we can find in Forty-ninth Street."

"But it's fine tonight, sir."

"Never mind; we can ask questions."

To make a long story short, they found three modern stores in the long block that had such floors. The first was a sandwich shop, the second a fancy fruiterer's and the third a high-class delicatessen. The sandwich shop did not use sawdust in rainy weather, but the other two did. There was a sack of the same kind of sawdust in the back of the delicatessen store. But the proprietors of both these stores insisted that they had never seen or served a person answering to the description of the man in the yellow overcoat.

"No luck!" Smither said dejectedly, as they came out of the delicatessen.

"Oh, I wouldn't say that," returned Lee. He was standing on the sidewalk, looking up at the windows over the store. Whoever had put in this modern store had not considered it worthwhile to recondition the rest of the house. It had a shabby air. "I didn't expect to find that the man dealt with these stores. They're too expensive."

"Then what was your object in asking, sir?"

"Just to give me a chance to look around. . . . Notice that the man who designed this store," he went on, "in order to get as much frontage as possible for the show window, put in the store door at the side. The little entry to the door has a nice tiled floor and of course the storekeeper would spread his sawdust on it, because that would be the spot to get most of the mud from the feet of the customers. But that little entry also leads to the door serving the upstairs part of the house. Look at that door, Smither."

It was a modern door in conformity with the rest of the store front. Inside the glass was pasted the word, Vacancy.

"Let's go up," said Lee.

He pressed the bell, and the door was opened by a push button from above. The landlady, a chronically suspicious woman like most of her profession, waited for them at the head of the stairs. She was surprised at the request of three prosperous-looking gentlemen to look at rooms at that hour, but proceeded to show them the best she had, a large, shabbily-furnished, second-floor front.

"Isn't this a very noisy street?" said Lee.

"Nothing out of the ordinary, sir. Only automobile traffic."

"I am a literary man. I must have quiet."

"I already have a literary gentleman, sir. He works here especial for the quiet. Top-floor hall. His home is in Jersey."

Lee's calm eye lighted up inwardly. Otherwise his face showed no change. "What does he write?" he asked idly.

"I couldn't tell you that, sir. He's a foreign gentleman, a Polack, I should say. Speaks broken. But always the gentleman."

"What's his name—not that it matters."

"Jan Dubinski, sir."

"Ah! Does he by chance wear a yellowish overcoat when he goes out?"

"Why, yes, sir! A foreign-made overcoat. So you know him!"

"Slightly. Can we trouble you to show us his room?"

"I can't do that, sir. He locks it when he goes out."

"But you must have a key in order to clean it."

"No, sir. He don't sleep here. He sweeps it himself when necessary."

"Then we must force the door. We are from the police department. We are interested in Mr. Dubinski. I will pay for any damage we do."

The Headquarters detective flashed his badge.

The woman's hand went to her mouth. "Oh dear! I don't want no trouble!" she murmured. "Such a quiet man!"

"Calm yourself," said Lee. "If this is the man we want, it doesn't reflect on you at all. Please show us the room."

She led the way up two more flights and pointed to a door in front. The detective rattled it. The old door was loose.

"I want a strong screwdriver," he said; "or a chisel, or any thin tool. A poker will do if you've got nothing better."

She fetched him a poker and he forced the door expertly.

"What was your profession before you joined the force?" asked Lee mildly.

Gumshoes didn't get it. "Truck-driver," he said without a smile.

This was a tiny room, the cheapest in the house. It contained a narrow bed, a scarred bureau, a kitchen table and chair by the window. The floor was covered with a dusty carpet having most of the nap worn off. On the table stood a typewriter, and Lee went to it straight. There were sheets of paper alongside; he put one in the machine and struck a few keys. The worn letters and the new exclamation point were instantly recognizable.

"This is the typewriter," said Lee, "and your lodger is the man we're looking for."

"Oh dear!" she said. "What's he done?"

Lee didn't want to give the woman a fit by mentioning murder. "I can't tell you. Read the papers." He pulled out the drawers in the bureau. They were perfectly empty. There was a shallow drawer in the table. Nothing there but more blank sheets of paper and carbon paper. "Look under the mattress," he said to Smither. "Feel under the carpet all over the room."

Smither having done so, shook his head.

"I have reason to believe he has something hidden here," insisted Lee.

""Where else is there to look, sir, in such a dump?"

"Examine the mattress," said Lee. "Make certain that it has not been ripped open and sewed up again." Meanwhile, with his magnifying glass, Lee was examining the woodwork of the room, door frame, baseboard, window frame and sill. The top-floor window in this old house was close to the floor. He discovered that the old paint in the cracks of the window sill was broken. "This board has been taken out at some time," he said. "See if you can pry it up with your poker, Officer."

The sill came up with unexpected ease. Beneath it, in the narrow space between laths and brick, a thin package wrapped in newspaper was standing on edge. Upon being opened, it was found to contain a carbon copy of the play "Sin," in the same worn type. Lee, who expected this, scarcely glanced at it. But in the hole there was also a long manila envelope, and he pounced on that. It contained a sheaf of letter-size sheets covered with miscellaneous typewritten notes. The first entries told Lee what a find he had made, and he smiled at last.

"This is worth all our trouble," he said softly to Smither. "With this we will send him to the chair!"

"We got to catch him first," said Smither gloomily. "What is it, sir?"

"The contents of Gavin Dordress' notebook. That notebook was missing after the murder. The murderer dared not keep the book itself, but he copied it out before destroying it. Notes for plots, for characters, for scenes. He needed that in the future."

"If the book is destroyed, can you prove in court that these notes came out of it?"

"I reckon so," said Lee, folding the papers. "I'll study the entries at my leisure. . . . Hello! here's something else." He drew out a small ruled sheet perforated along one edge. "A page from the notebook itself! So much the better!"

"What funny-looking writing!" said Smither, looking over Lee's shoulder. "It's a kind of puzzle, isn't it? I can't make nothing of it."

"He couldn't, either," said Lee. "And he saved it until he could. He thought, because this one entry was written in cipher, that it must be especially important to him. Maybe it is. I'll have a try at deciphering it when I get home."

He returned the papers to the envelope, and stowed the envelope carefully in his breast pocket. "That will be all," he said cheerfully.

"We will have to carry away all these papers; also the typewriter. The officer will give you a formal receipt for them, ma'am. . . . And please accept this from me for your trouble."

It was a twenty-dollar bill. The astonished woman stammered her thanks. She was not prepared for such liberality from the police.

From the delicatessen store Lee called up Headquarters. "Loasby," he said, "you have Hillman, Gavin Dordress' former butler, under surveillance?"

"I have."

"Can you get in touch with the man who is watching him?"

"In two minutes."

"Good. I'm about to telephone Hillman to ask him to come to my apartment. If he comes, all right. If he tries to escape, he's to be arrested instantly."

"I get you, Lee. Want me up there?"

"Yes, please. I have important new evidence. Give Hillman time to get downtown first. Bring the old Gladstone bag and its contents."

"Right. Be at your place in three-quarters of an hour."

Lee then called the Harvest Restaurant in the Bronx. Hillman himself answered the phone. "Hillman," said Lee, "could you oblige me by coming down to my apartment?"

After a silence Hillman said nervously: "Why, certainly, Mr. Mappin. I'll get my wife to relieve me here. Am I to come to the front door or the service entrance, sir?"

"The front door," said Lee, "Take a taxi."

CHAPTER THIRTY

THE THREE MEN taxied over to the East River. The theaters were not yet out and they made good time. Driving through the streets, they could hear newsboys calling extras with the latest news of the attack on Cynthia Dordress and the search for the man in the yellow overcoat. Lee, thoughtfully rolling an unlighted cigar between his lips, stared out of the window the whole way without seeing anything.

When the cab drew up in front of his house he glanced at his two companions. "You boys had better come up with me. I may need you."

They entered the house. There was another Headquarters man waiting in the lobby. The two detectives passed each other without any sign of recognition. Upstairs, when Jermyn opened the door, Lee heard a murmur of men's voices in the distant living-room, and his face hardened.

"Who's here?" he whispered.

"Mr. Townley, Mr. Gundy, and Mr. Ackroyd."

Lee's eyebrows went up. "I told you not to let anybody in the apartment!"

"But your intimate friends, sir," protested Jermyn. "They said they'd wait until you returned. I didn't like to take it on myself to . . ."

Lee smoothed his ruffled feathers. "All right. . . . Have they seen Miss Cynthia?"

"No, sir. I told them she was indisposed. The young ladies are together in the guest-room."

175

"Did the men come together or singly?"

"Singly, sir. Mr. Townley came first."

"Put this typewriter out of sight under your bed. Take these two gentlemen through the kitchen into your room. Feed them, if they're hungry, and give them a drink. Keep your voices down. I don't want anybody to know they're here."

"Yes, sir."

The three men disappeared silently through the pantry door; Lee proceeded through the long gallery. His vast square living-room was lined on two sides with windows looking east over the river and south over the town. Here Lee's guests waited.

"Lee!" they cried out together, all starting for him. Siebert with long strides reached him first. All three talked at once, asking about Cynthia.

Lee waved his hands. "One at a time! . . . Cynthia is not injured except for a bruise or two. But she has had a nasty shock. The man has not been caught, but the police have hopes."

"Could I see her!" pleaded Emmett. "I know it's a lot to ask. But if I could see her only for a moment."

Seibert glared at him angrily, and Emmett turned his back on him. The mere presence of Siebert in the same room always made the carefully arranged Emmett look his age. Emmett knew it, and it made him vicious. He glanced in a convenient mirror and stroked his mustache. That, at least, looked young.

"I expect she's gone to bed," Lee said mildly. "But I'll find out. You boys will have to excuse me for a few moments. A cable has come that I must decode." Lee went to the bookshelves and abstracted a thin volume, much worn. "My code book," he said pleasantly. He took care to conceal the cover of the book under his arm as he went out.

Lee entered a little study that adjoined his bed-room, and seating himself at the desk, switched on a lamp. The book under his arm was a manual of the language of the ancient Phœnicians. Opening it at the page illustrating the Phœnician alphabet, he laid the leaf from Gavin Dordress' notebook beside it, and started to translate it on another sheet. The first words gave him a clue to the whole. His jaw dropped; he stared incredulously at the page, then went on putting down the modern characters rapidly.

Alone in his own room with the door shut, he had no need of putting a guard on his face. Amazement, horror, and a grim satisfaction succeeded each other there. He finished the last letter with a stab of his pencil, and seizing original and translation, jumped up and, slipping them in his pocket, started back for the living-room. At the door of the study a new thought came to him. Turning in the other direction, he knocked on Cynthia's door. His face was as expressionless as wood then. Cynthia was awake; the two girls were talking quietly. Lee, when it suited him, could lie as smoothly as any man in Christendom. When Fanny opened the door, he said:

"I've just had a telephone message. The man has been caught." Cynthia's face flushed very pink, and paled again. "Thank God!" she said. "Then he can do no further harm."

Fanny, studying Lee, said nothing. She knew her employer better than Cynthia did.

"If I have him brought here," said Lee, "do you feel able to face him for the purpose of identification?"

"Why, certainly," Cynthia said quickly. "I'm all right. I want to do my part. I'll get dressed at once."

"No need of that," said Lee. "Dressing-gown and slippers will do. You will only be wanted for a moment. I'll let you know."

As he was leaving them he heard the bell ring and when he got out into the corridor Jermyn was at the door. The visitor was not Hillman nor Loasby, whom Lee expected, but a veiled woman. He saw Jermyn start back. The woman, catching sight of Lee, pushed past the servant, throwing her veil back. It was Gail Garrett. So broken was she, so haggard, so careless in her dress, that Lee did not recognize her until she had almost reached him. She appeared to be almost beside herself.

"Lee! That ghastly story in the papers. How is the girl? I could not rest until I had found out."

The once glorious voice had a raucous edge on it; her utterance was slurred as if she had been drinking or was under the influence of a drug. Lee looked at her in grim pity. "Cynthia's all right," he said. He stepped to the door of the living-room and closed it.

Gail clapped her hands to her head. "O God, Lee! do you think I hired that brute to kill Gavin, and then attack the girl? I cannot bear my life! I cannot bear it!"

Lee shook his head. "Once I may have had that possibility in mind. I know better now."

She dropped in a chair against the wall of the gallery and drew the back of her hand across the forehead, staring. "Lee, let me see the girl for a moment. Just a little moment. Let me go down on my knees and beg her to forgive me. She couldn't refuse! She's a woman, too. She has a heart. O God, Lee! I loved him so! I can't bear my life! Let me see the girl."

Lee shook his head. "It wouldn't do any good. You must remember she knows you plotted to kill her father. That's not easy to forgive. Better leave it to time."

Gail got to her feet unsteadily. "Oh, well, it doesn't matter. I'm done for. I've got no friends."

"I'll look you up when I get this business out of the way," said Lee. "Something can be done."

She was on her way to the door. "Don't bother," she said.

The bell had rung again, and Jermyn was opening the door. This was Hillman, the ex-butler. At sight of him Gail cried out sharply.

"What are you doing here? Are you following me? Is this a trap?"

The gaunt Hillman, terrified at the sight of her, turned as if to run, but Jermyn was at the door behind him, blocking the way. "No, no, Miss," he stammered. "I didn't expect to find you here."

"I don't care," said Gail recklessly. "My money's all gone. You can't get another cent out of me. So publish and be damned!"

"No, Miss, no!" protested Hillman.

Lee, sharply interested, came forward. "Publish what?" he asked.

"My letters. Last year I wrote some indiscreet letters to Gavin. He tore them up and threw them in his waste-basket. This worm recovered the pieces and, putting them together, started blackmailing me by threatening to sell the letters to a tabloid. When he got the notion of starting a restaurant I had to pay him thousands."

"So that's why you paid!" murmured Lee. "Well, I'll be damned! It had nothing to do with Gavin's death!"

"No! This was before," said Gail impatiently. She turned on Hillman again. "Go ahead and sell the letters. You can't do me any further harm."

"No," whined human. "I want you to have the letters. I been twice to your hotel to give them to you, but they wouldn't let me see you. I didn't dare trust them to a servant. Here, Miss, here!" He was offering her a little packet wrapped in paper.

Gail stared at him uncertainly; took the packet; opened one end of it; pulled out a letter; counted the rest; and thrust the packet in her handbag. "It's too late," she muttered. "These can't help me."

Lee was angry. "Well, by God! that restaurant is rightfully yours," he said.

Hillman faced him in terror. "No! No! Mr. Mappin," he cried sharply. "If you take it from me it will be no good to nobody! I'll pay! I'll pay her every cent I got off her. I'll pay a hundred a week, maybe more later."

Gail cursed him.

"Take it!" Lee urged her. "Go to a sanatorium and recover your health; make a come-back on the stage. You have plenty of friends; you are not forgotten."

Gail shrugged indifferently. "It's not worth the trouble. Life is too tedious to endure!"

She went on to the door, and Jermyn let her out.

"Just the same, I'll hold you to that promise," Lee said sternly to Hillman. "A hundred dollars a week to Miss Garrett. The first week you default you'll be clapped in jail."

"Oh, Mr. Mappin, I will never default!" cowed Hillman. "I want to do the right thing. Mr. Mappin, I went into this business very unwillingly. Nobody knows how I suffered while it was going on."

"You took the money."

"I'm not a bad man, Mr. Mappin."

"There might be two opinions about that."

"It was my wife forced me to do it. She's ambitious."

"You can go," said Lee.

Hillman did not immediately obey. "Mr. Mappin, was it for this reason that you sent for me?"

"No. I knew nothing about your blackmailing operations until now."

"Why did you want to see me, Mr. Mappin?"

"Well," said Lee grimly, "I had a notion to try an overcoat on you, but I've learned since I phoned you that it doesn't fit."

After Hillman left, Lee entered the living-room with a wooden face. "Sorry to keep you boys waiting," he said. "I had a visitor."

"That's all right," they murmured variously.

"Cynthia had gone to bed. But she said she'd come in for a minute. You'd better wait."

"That's splendid!" said Emmett.

"Bea will feel better if I can take her a first-hand report," said Mack.

Siebert said nothing.

Lee was deeply excited. He surreptitiously wiped his face. His ears were stretched for the sound of the doorbell. He kept glancing at his watch. Why the hell didn't Loasby come? No one could have guessed from his mild face that he was churning inside.

Emmett, to fill the uncomfortable pause, asked Mack how business was at the theater.

"Couldn't be better," growled Mack. "Fifty or more standees nightly. At every matinee we turn hundreds away."

"It's the title that attracts the women," said Emmett.

At last the sound of the doorbell. Lee stood up. He heard the rumble of Loasby's deep voice in the gallery, and presently the Inspector entered, carrying the old scuffed Gladstone bag. Lee introduced him.

"This is Inspector Loasby, gentlemen. Mr. Gundy, Mr. Ackroyd. Mack Townley you know."

Hands were shaken all around. Lee watched the faces.

"By God!" said Mack. "Is that the bag the fellow left in the lavatory? Let's see what's in it, Inspector."

The bag was opened out flat on a table and the shapeless yellow overcoat taken out and exhibited—the curious leather helmet; the rumpled suit; broken shoes; spectacles. There was a small tin make-up box with sticks of grease paint, cold cream, etc. Lee, glancing in the faces bending over these things, could see nothing showing there but simple curiosity. He said:

"Notice how cleverly the shoulders and back of the overcoat have been padded to alter the wearer's figure."

"Then he wasn't such a big fellow, after all," said Mack.

"Tall," remarked Lee. "One of you fellows try it on."

"I'm damned if I will!" said Siebert.

"Maybe it's lousy," said Mack, drawing back.

"Nothing doing!" said Emmett.

Lee looked Emmett up and down speculatively. "Seems as if it was about your size. Try it on."

"No. Put it on yourself."

"I'm too little," said Lee. He glanced at Loasby.

"Put it on, Mr. Gundy," barked the Inspector in his official voice.

Emmett's face turned greenish. "Well, if you insist," he said with a ghastly grin. He wriggled into the overcoat, and Lee noted how snugly the padding fitted over his shoulders and back. They pulled the leather helmet over his head. The thick glasses changed his whole expression.

"This dirty-looking grease paint was to make his face cadaverous," said Lee. He started rubbing it into Emmett's cheeks. "Brown for an unshaven chin. I can't take the time to make a perfect job of this, but it will give you an idea."

"Don't mind me," said Emmett, bringing out a laugh. "Always glad to afford amusement to my friends."

Lee noted that he was breathing as quick as a wounded animal; and saw how the sweat oozed through the grease paint on his face. Emmett was grinning like a man on the rack. Lee unobtrusively pressed a button in the wall. Returning, he added a few finishing touches to his work.

"What have I got to do?" asked Emmett, laughing. "Act in a charade?"

Nobody answered him.

When Lee heard Jermyn coming in the gallery he went to meet him at the door of the room and told him in a low tone to ask Miss Cynthia to come in. Afterwards he was to fetch out the two men from his room and let them wait in the gallery until wanted.

"Now can I take off this rig?" asked Emmett.

"In a minute," said Lee.

Cynthia came in quickly, followed by Fanny. Cynthia was wearing a blue cashmere negligee of Fanny's, trimmed with swansdown, which gave her an ethereal appearance. Every man in the room caught his breath at the sight of her. Having been warned, she was not startled at the sight of the man in the yellow overcoat. She looked him up and down gravely. Emmett turned rigid at the sight of her. His hand stole to his throat. He seemed to be trying to speak, and could not.

"Is this the man who attacked you this evening?" asked Loasby.

"I think so," she said doubtfully. "There is something different about him. . . . No, Inspector, this man has a mustache and that other had a shaven lip."

"Pardon me," said Lee. "I forgot that." He turned to Emmett. The latter threw an arm over his mouth, but Loasby pulled down both his arms from behind and held them. The trim little mustache came away in Lee's hand with a couple of pulls. "It's false," he said. "In disguising himself he reversed the usual procedure. Rather clever of him."

"That is the man," said Cynthia. "I am certain of it now."

Fanny slipped an arm through Cynthia's and the two girls went out.

"I can produce a dozen more identifying witnesses," murmured Lee.

There was a silence in the big room. Siebert and Mack were staring at Emmett, dazed. Loasby was the first to speak. He said, with a curious mixture of admiration and chagrin:

"Nice work, Lee. Like the Mounties, you always get your man."

Lee, with a look of pain, threw up his hand. "This was more than just another case, Inspector."

No sound came from Emmett. Loasby had released his arms. Suddenly, with the quickness of an animal, he sprang for the open window. The river was two hundred feet below. Loasby grabbed him, but he slipped through. Siebert thrust out a foot and he crashed to the ground. They seized him. He struggled silently, like a madman, with the strength of three. Loasby drew his gun and, reversing it, struck him on the head with the butt. Emmett went limp. Smither and the Headquarters detective ran in.

"Have you got handcuffs?" Loasby asked his man.

"Yes, sir."

"Put them on him, and carry him out into the gallery. Phone down to the lobby for Williamson to come up. Get a car to take this fellow to Headquarters."

Again there was a silence in the big room. The men looked at each other, unable to comprehend that it was all over. Siebert murmured: "Gavin was Emmett's friend for twenty-five years!" After a moment, he added: "I can't seem to get it straight, Lee. What about the play?"

"It was Gavin's play. That's what Emmett killed him for. Emmett copied it, making a few unimportant changes, and sent it to you under the name of John Venner."

"Good God, Lee! Do you blame me for my part in marketing it?"

"Did you know it was Gavin's play?"

"No! I'm not a literary man. I'm an agent!"

"That lets you out." Lee looked at Mack somberly. "Mack knew it."

Mack's face turned livid. "No, Lee!" he cried.

"Don't lie," said Lee deprecatingly. "I have proof that you knew."

"How could I have known it? I only surmised it."

"Why didn't you tell me before you put it into rehearsal?"

"That wouldn't have brought Gavin back."

"It would have saved me two months' work, and Cynthia all that mental agony. . . . Suppose this brute had killed her this evening?"

Mack flung an arm up. "For God's sake don't speak of that, Lee! Try to put yourself in my place," he went on. "This play gave me my only chance to effect a reconciliation with Bea. She was mad to nose out the Garrett woman and play that part."

"Sure," said Lee. "And what was friendship?"

Mack was silent.

"Lee," asked Loasby, "how did you pin it on Emmett Gundy?"

"We traced him by the old typewriter. Tonight we found the hangout where he did his typing. In a hole in the, wall I found a page from Gavin's notebook which Emmett had saved because he couldn't read it, and he thought it must be important. It was important. It'll send him to the chair." Lee took the leaf from his pocket and passed it over.

"This is all in hieroglyphics," said Loasby.

"Phœnician characters," corrected Lee. "When we were in school together Gavin and I used to correspond in these characters in order to conceal our boyish secrets. There are only nineteen letters in the Phoenician alphabet and when we lacked a letter we turned one of our own upside down. Gavin had occasion to make an entry in his notebook that he didn't want anybody to read, and he naturally turned to these characters again."

"What does it say?" asked Loasby.

"Listen." Lee read slowly:

"For his new novel Emmett said he needed a farewell letter left by a successful man who had suddenly tired of life. He couldn't seem to get it right, and I wrote out a draft for him. Afterwards the amusing thought came to me: Suppose E. were to kill me and leave this letter beside my body? There's an idea for a crime play in this."

"Good God!" murmured Siebert.

The police took away their prisoner. Mack Townley and Smither went, and so Siebert was left with Lee. It was plain to Lee that Siebert was more than anxious to see Cynthia before he left.

Lee said, "Well, if I could trust you merely to say goodnight . . ."

Siebert didn't need any more of a hint. He made for her bed-room with four-foot strides.

When Fanny opened the door he said breathlessly; "Just wanted to say good-night to Cynthia." Fanny, smiling, opened the door wide, and there she lay. "Cynthia!" he murmured, forgetting every-thing.

He flung his arms around her. It turned out to be a long kiss. Cynthia relaxed and her white arms stole around his neck.

"I love you so much!" he murmured.

"I suppose I love you, too," Cynthia answered. "But, Lord, you're going to be difficult to manage!"

CHAPTER THIRTY-ONE

AFTER HIS ARREST Emmett Gundy appeared to turn completely apathetic, but those who visited him reported that there was a wicked fire hidden in the man. He said he had no money to employ a lawyer, and he rejected all offers to supply him with one. Lee would have been glad to contribute to such a cause, merely for the sake of seeing justice done. A famous alienist interested himself in the case, but Emmett would not submit to an examination. In the end the court assigned one of the thousand-dollar men to defend him. This lawyer could get nothing out of his client. Emmett insisted on pleading guilty, and no doubt the lawyer encouraged it because it saved him trouble. In any case, the evidence for the prosecution was overwhelming.

When it was all over it transpired that Emmett had left a confession. It was a strange document. Instead of expressing sorrow for his acts, he appeared to glory in them.

"I had had it in for Gavin Dordress for a long time," he wrote. "Every time he gave me money I hated him, because I should have been the one to give money to him. He had everything in the world; fame, money, lovers, friends, and I had nothing. It wasn't fair, because when we were young men together everybody said I had more talent than he. But he was crafty; he had the art of getting what he wanted out of people. Everybody fell for him. I wasn't liked because I was too honest. He had no real talent; his plays weren't any good, but he was a past master of publicity. He milked other men's brains; some of his best ideas he stole from me. My novels

were so good, the publishers were afraid of them. There was a con-
spiracy to keep me down.

"It was his secretiveness that gave me the idea of rubbing him
out. He would never tell anybody what he was writing. As soon as
I made sure of this, I began to lay my plans to get his play. Sitting
in his studio one day, looking out of the window, I saw how easy it
would be to come down from the roof of the building next door.
Every time I went into the sunroom I saw the key to the garden
door hanging there, and I knew that nobody went out in the garden after summer was over. So one day I prigged the key and had a
duplicate made. Afterwards I returned the original key to its place
without its ever having been missed. I got the suicide letter out of
him a couple of weeks before I was ready to use it.

"I spent a lot of thought and time on my disguise. As I would
have to pass through the next building, firstly to get the lay of the
land, and secondly to pull the trick, I had to make myself look completely different from my usual self. At first I couldn't see through
the thick glasses I put on, but I trained myself so that I could look
around them. I shaved off my mustache and practiced with false
hair until I could apply one exactly like it. Thus I was able to go
clean shaven when disguised.

"My opportunity came on the night Gavin gave a dinner party,
I left the party early, changed to my disguise in the Penn Station,
and got to the roof of the building next door. I lowered myself to
Gavin's roof garden by means of a thin, strong rope ladder I had
made. I could see into the penthouse through the windows. Hillman
was still there and I waited. Meanwhile I took off my disguise. I
had on a black overcoat under the yellow one and a hat in the
pocket, and I fixed up to look like my ordinary self as well as I
could in the dark.

"As soon as Gavin was alone I let myself into the sun-room,
crossed the lobby, and went out into the elevator hall without
his hearing me. I had a little mirror, and in the hall I fixed my
mustache. All these details were planned in advance. I rang the
apartment bell. Gavin came to the door. He was surprised to see
me back. I told him I was so nervous I couldn't sleep; I wanted

somebody to talk to. He couldn't very well turn me away. He took me in the studio and offered me a drink. While he was away getting ice I put a glove on, and got his gun out of the desk drawer and dropped it in my pocket. I kept my gloved hand out of sight. He suggested a game of chess to quiet my nerves. This suited me all right. While he was sitting in his chair arranging the men on a little tabourette in front of him, I came up at one side and shot him.

"I took my time to fix everything. In a drawer of his desk I found the script of an old play. The fire was about out. I burned the script page by page to make sure it was completely destroyed, and then laid the half-burned title page of 'The Changeling' on the hearth. I strapped the rest of 'The Changeling' script around my waist. I put away the chessmen and moved the tabourette. I laid the farewell letter on his desk, left the lights burning, and got out. Resumed my disguise in the garden; climbed the rope ladder and pulled it up after me; tied it around me under the overcoat. I had a little difficulty getting out of the building next door, because it was closed up for the night, but by listening carefully, I could keep tab of the watchman on his rounds, and I finally made my way down to the ground floor and let myself out into the street.

"Amos Lee Mappin, being an intimate friend of Gavin's, was the greatest danger I ran, but I had to chance it. Mappin is a slippery customer, and a criminal at heart. He always had it in for me. The police were satisfied as to suicide; they never figured in the case until the end. Only Mappin insisted that it was murder; he saw good publicity in it for himself. I made Louella Kip swear to an alibi for me that night. She never knew that I had put Gavin out. She just thought she was saving me inconvenience.

"When I read that Mappin had found a little bruise on Gavin's forehead and had sketched it, I was worried. I knew Gavin must have got it from striking against one of the chessmen, and I expected Mappin would find the chessmen next. I thought there might be a speck of blood or skin on one of them. So I assumed my disguise and returned to the penthouse that night. When I got down to the roof of the lower building, I found to my surprise that Mappin and the girl were staying in the apartment, but that didn't frighten me off. I waited until they went to bed, and let myself in and re-placed the chessmen with a different set. On the way out the girl saw me in the dark and screamed, but luck was with me. She fainted, and while Mappin was bringing her to, I made a getaway.

"The rest is pretty well known. Everything went wrong after the play was produced. The girl made believe to recognize the play as Gavin's work. She couldn't have known it was his play; it was only a notion that she insisted on. And Mappin backed her up, of course. So I was unable to cash in on my royalties. I had to give up my room at the Vanderveer. In the first place, if Gavin's death had been accepted as a suicide, I had intended to come out after a bit, and acknowledge the play as mine. Then I could have lived easy for the rest of my life. But Mappin spoiled all that. It was only by a fluke that he caught me in the end. My plans were perfect. But I was too daring in going to his apartment that night.

"Emmett Gundy"

COACHWHIP PUBLICATIONS

COACHWHIPBOOKS.COM

1

HULBERT FOOTNER
THE ADVENTURES OF
MADAME STOREY

ISBN 978-1-61646-236-9

THE MURDER
THAT HAD
EVERYTHING!

HULBURT
FOOTNER

ISBN 978-1-61646-258-2

COACHWHIP PUBLICATIONS

COACHWHIPBOOKS.COM

THE
MYSTERY
OF THE
FOLDED
PAPER

HULBERT
FOOTNER

ISBN 978-1-61646-255-8

ORCHIDS TO MURDER

HULBERT FOOTNER

ISBN 978-1-61646-262-8

COACHWHIP PUBLICATIONS

COACHWHIPBOOKS.COM

WHO KILLED THE
HUSBAND?

HULBERT FOOTNER

ISBN 978-1-61646-256-6

CLUES AND CORPSES
The Detective Fiction and
Mystery Criticism of Todd Downing
CURTIS EVANS

ISBN 978-1-61646-145-4

Coachwhip Publications

CoachwhipBooks.com

THE LAST
TRUMPET
A HUGH RENNERT MYSTERY

TODD DOWNING

ISBN 978-1-61646-152-2

COACHWHIP PUBLICATIONS

COACHWHIPBOOKS.COM

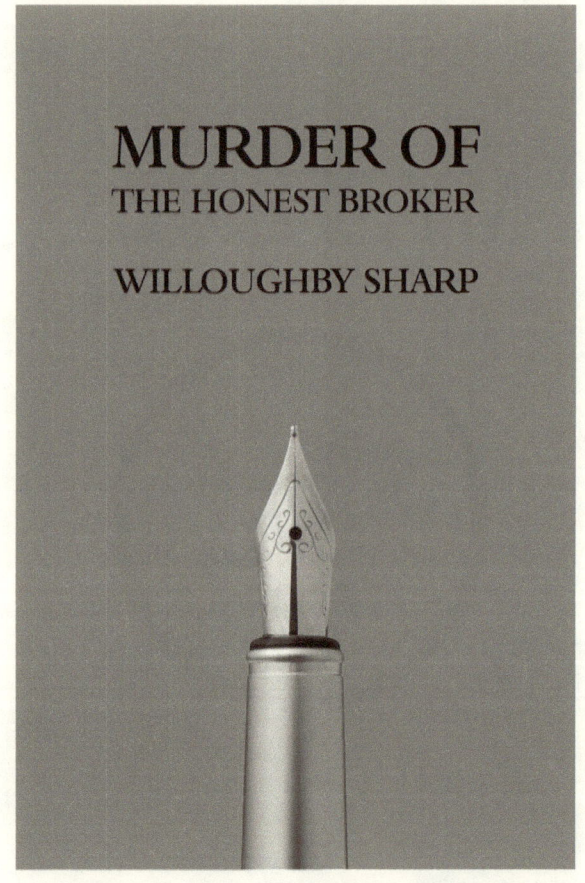

MURDER OF
THE HONEST BROKER

WILLOUGHBY SHARP

ISBN 978-1-61646-211-6

www.ingramcontent.com/pod-product-compliance
Lightning Source LLC
Chambersburg PA
CBHW031234260626
47169CB00007B/2290